CATFIGHT

K. T. Waltzer

ISBN-10: 0615615147
ISBN-13: 978-0615615141

For Richard

Jacket design and illustration by Outer Margins Design

What we've got here is failure to communicate.
-Frank Pierson

ONE

"WE'RE EVERY ETHNIC MAFIA'S desert of choice, but the local law don't care about that, cuz the dead don't cause no trouble. Other than requiring a respectable disposal. We don't see too many like you around here. You're the one that got away.

"Now that we know where you're from, we can get after Los Angeles again. When you were first brought in, we told them we got a real live comatose Jane Doe. But they never followed up. Lordy. And it's been weeks now. Since you're doing better, we contacted them again the other day, but who knows when that LA County will ever come out to this no man's land, even though we're just a quick fifty mile hop northeast of Needles. You just know those lazy-asses think that when they get here, they'll have to deal with all the carcasses piling up in this God-forsaken place. Well, we can't do their work for them. See, we got enough going on with the prison here— now don't get all freaky-like on me. I ain't doing no time for nothin' heavy. Some of us inmates here pull double duty as hospital staff. The ambulance that picked you up, for example, it was manned by cons, but just the ones on good behavior. We call them the A Team. That's A as in ambulance..."

The patient, flat-backed in bed, packed with dope and almost dead, stared at the ceiling. Corporal Klinger would not shut up.

"...Doc's a con, too. He's doing life for double murder. Even though his license was revoked, he cut a deal to practice with us, because non-con docs won't come here."

1

The nurses' aide left the patient's side to grab a stool from the hallway, wheeled it back into the room and flipped the lights on. An army of shiny cockroaches advanced into the sterile terrain, leaving the only other intruder in the room the oppressive drone of the overhead fluorescents. Rolling the stool up to the bed, the aide straddled the seat and leaned in close.

"Time to get back to business. Remember how we blinked to communicate the other day? We are going to do it again. Once for no and twice for yes," he reminded the patient. "Understand?"

The patient blinked twice.

"Now, about the letter I've been helping you with. We're almost done. Tell me if it works for you:

'Dear so and so'—I'll get their name later as I said— *'I am in critical but stable condition at Mojave Medical Center in Bullhead City. I was beat up and almost died. Someone found me. I was in a coma and am just now coming out of it. I am slowly getting bits and pieces of my memory back. I can't speak yet. My skull was smashed and my arms are broken. As you know, the little family I have, I'm estranged from. By the time you get this, I should be ready to...'* well, that's it so far," he said.

A lone blink toward the ceiling.

"Okay. What would you like to change?" the aide asked, keeping his eye on the patient as he reached for the blink chart.

Blink.

"You don't want to change it. Do you want to add to it?"

Blink. Blink.

Holding up the alphabet chart, the aide began running his long, slender, expertly manicured fingers slowly across the block lettering, noting every blink with a jot of his pen on the legal pad. After a few minutes he looked at what he had put together.

"*'I know what you did,*'" he read aloud. He looked at the patient, who had just drifted back into the sea of the unconscious.

"Strange way to end a note. Lordy. But I am no one to pass judgment."

TWO

Six months earlier

I T WAS LOUD. It got her attention. It stole her concentration, robbing her of an all night design-think. She looked up from the drafting table, vision bleary from focusing in bad lighting and looked toward the front door. As she walked from the kitchen that temporarily doubled as her studio, and maneuvered through stacks of yet-to-be unpacked boxes through the living room where the door came in to view, it was obvious that this wasn't your everyday knock. Someone was beating the shit out of the front door.

She was confused. She had no idea who it could be because she had just moved into the ground floor of the loft five days before and hadn't met any neighbors. Not only that, but her watch said it was 7:30 am. She held it to her ear and was reassured to hear it ticking. It was too early for anyone she knew to come by unannounced.

As she looked toward the door again, an open box of framed photographs of her recently former life blocked her line of sight. As her eyes locked contact with his, it hit her. It had to be Michael. She stopped briefly and ran her fingers over the photo of her ex. Her heart raced, she bit her lip and went to answer the door. Maybe it is him, she thought. Maybe he's changed his mind about the divorce.

"Who's there?" Emily Everheart yelled, which was the only way one could be heard over the noise. The loud knocking ended the moment she yelled, but no one answered.

"Michael?" Still no response. She placed her ear to the door, wishing she had an eyehole to look through— one more thing to add to her to-do list. Someone was definitely there; she could hear whomever it was fidgeting about on the stoop. The chain was still in its lock, which allowed Emily to open the door only a tight couple of inches. As she did this, a slice of intense morning light burst into her entry, blinding her. When her eyes adjusted a few seconds later, she found herself looking eye to eye with a pair of oversized glasses. Emily's heart jumped into her throat and she slammed the door. It's definitely not Michael, she thought. Breathing hard, she backed up against the door. "What do you want?" she yelled over her shoulder.

"Did I forget to tell you I was coming by?" the singsong voice chirped. "I live upstairs."

Relieved, but annoyed, Emily caught her breath and pried open the door as far as the chain would go and peered guardedly into the face of this unknown person.

"I'm Candy. Candy Jones," the neighbor said, still upbeat as she extended her hand through the opening. Emily did not return the gesture. "I'm sorry to bother you, but I wanted to introduce myself. I didn't want you thinking, who is this rude neighbor of mine? and such. Hey, I hear you're divorced—"

"What?" Emily blurted out, cutting her off. "How would you know such a thing? No, never mind, it's none of your business," Emily said, appalled this woman would have the nerve to say such a thing. Even though the divorce was Emily's idea, it had left her deeply wounded and constantly battling bouts of raw emotion. It was a touchy subject and she could barely think about it without becoming agitated. And now, right here in her own home was this insufferable, Candy Jones, chatting away about Emily's divorce like it was the weather.

"Oh, just teasing you. Heck, you're sensitive. Let me make it up to you," Candy Jones said, tilting her head to one side, smiling warmly. "Come on up for coffee and cheese Danish. Kathie Lee's on soon! We'll have a blast. I think she has the grandkids on today!"

"Look, Candy, I'm on a deadline. I've been up all night working in metric and quite frankly I just can't take the time. But thank you," Emily said flatly as she started to close the door.

"Well, Candy doesn't take no for an answer," Candy said as she stuck her foot in the door. "How about tonight? Come up for a drink."

"I'll be working through the night again. Besides, I don't drink," Emily lied, thinking this woman would get the hint. Candy Jones was really rubbing her every wrong way. Emily could feel any patience she once had heading fast for point zero.

"Oh, I gotcha. Got a little to close to the Chardonnay. I completely understand," Candy said not only with her foot in the door but her face too, creepily reminiscent of Nicholson's iconic "HERE'S JOHNNY!"

Emily couldn't believe her ears. Without wasting another breath on this conversation she abruptly shut the door. In doing so, the door chafed Candy's cheek and knocked off her glasses.

Candy backed away from the door, snickering mixed with the odd snort, picked up her glasses and headed back to her place. A heavy stepper, she stomped her way up the stairs, each step a racket compounding the next. As Candy let herself back into her apartment, Emily wondered why she hadn't noticed her loud neighbor before this.

Somewhat calmed down and back to work, Emily studied a problem area of the floor plan she had been trying, without success, to resolve. She had designed a very well thought-out public space, but the client was having problems with the reception area. The client's pornographic sculpture collection was to be displayed prominently throughout the space. Emily had designed a freestanding gallery, out of the way, so as not to offend the more conservative clients who would be passing through the space. The client, a man little in stature but who stood on scads of inherited money, had awful taste. Needless to say, he didn't go for her discreet first pass at the gallery area. He was insisting on built-in niches as well as free-standing pedestals placed front and center, so that all the people passing through the space could experience the *art* the way it was meant to be experienced. More important, the center of each sculpture had to be viewed at eye level. Emily was growing frustrated. She never would have accepted a request for this type of proposal in the past, but the dreary reality was that she wasn't in any place to turn down work. She had taken a hiatus from work since her marriage had come to an end and she was living on funds pared down more than any minimalist interior. Since happiness had eluded her for sometime now, hunting down work was a positive distraction in helping to get her life back on the right road.

Right now though, Emily was running on fumes. Any artistic fuel that she held in reserve was now burned up by that energy-guzzling hog Candy. Since she was out of her little helper *Adderall*, she needed something to restart her imaginative engine.

Her desk was a mess and that didn't help. She needed a clean worktop in order to gather her thoughts. She moved a stack of sketches off to the left side. She picked up the Zen Kitten and Puppy calendar— a thank you from an animal rescue fund for a generous donation— and placed it on top of the sketches. She turned it over so her heartstrings would be shielded from gentle tugs by perky little fluffy faces, but in doing so, she found herself gazing into the innocent eyes of a darling little kitten curled up in a teacup, looking up lovingly at her from the backside of the calendar.

Pushing forward, she took the roll of sketch paper and pulled off a few pieces. She flattened the sketch paper over one of the floor plans and was laying out new locations for the porno niches when the phone rang. Only a few people knew that unlisted number, but even so, whoever it was would have to wait. She let the voice mail pick up. Her deadline was in just over twenty-four hours, and she hoped she could get some sleep between now and then. She traced a new outline of the design on the flimsy paper. She backed off for a minute to evaluate it. Having no choice at this point but to be amenable to her client's wishes, she also decided there was no way she would put her name on this project. If she were awarded the project, she would take the money and flee.

Her mind drifted back to Michael. How could she have been so stupid! That was probably him trying to call! Of course he wants to talk to her. She reached over to the phone and hit the voice mail button.

"It's me. I hope I didn't offend you. I like a drink or two myself. I always get a laugh when I hear of those blackouts and all that puking. I didn't mean to bushwhack you earlier. Please accept my apology. Tell you what, let me cook dinner tonight and I'll bring it down to you, since you're too busy to come up here. I'll be there at seven thirty."

Emily Everheart stared at the phone, then stared up at the ceiling. How her neighbor was able to find this unlisted number unsettled her. Her jaw dropped open with shock. Furthermore, how could someone, an adult especially, be so ignorant? Talk about a barrel of misplaced confidence. She took three deep *sama vritti* breaths, and let go of her bothersome neighbor.

She had erased any suggestion of Candy and her offensive words, until *bushwhack* flew back into her thoughts, circled to and fro, then landed in the part of her brain where one stockpiles negligible information and subconscious cues, thus illuminating the light bulb in her head which reactivated her creative spark. Her eyes searched the desktop and she hastily leafed through her sketches and found what she was looking for. She pulled out the previous morning's crossword and looked at the clue that had stumped her: *ensnare*. So obvious now! Emily block lettered B U S H W H A C K in the unfilled squares. Pleased at this, she was able to justify that the intrusion had some minor purpose. Few things were better than the secret satisfaction of completing the last corner of a puzzle. For some reason, the elation she experienced from finishing, allowed her to believe she could tackle anything. Now, feeling refreshed, she knew she'd finish her project on time.

As she looked back down on her revised sketch, she realized she needed to cross-reference an area on an elevation. Bringing the diagram she needed up on her display, and focusing on the entire floor plan instead of just the lobby, she noticed that in plan view the lobby area stuck out prominently. Although she had designed it otherwise, the end result looked like a very large erect penis. She gasped. It hadn't been intentional. Really.

THREE

FLOUR DUSTED THE KITCHEN. The richness of an exotic vanilla perfumed the air. Candy Jones, a precision pastry chef, baked superhuman quantities of extreme cakes and monster pies at home for the chicest of restaurants and food boutiques all over the Westside of L.A. She had debuted on the dessert scene with the tall, preening, four layer cake dressed in seductive floral frosting. So breathtaking these creations, that people spent hours overanalyzing her technique via the baking blogs.

Her pies were gussied-up with goodies and had been just as much in demand as the cakes. Not a soggy crust, not a drizzle of fruit trespassing down the side of a pan, not a singed edge would ever appear in any of her pies.

Lately, though, the epic Dessert Channel battles and sweeping cupcake wars had commandeered the sweet-eaters' hankerings and had made her rethink her strategy. So her most recent creations were miniature sizes of an entire cake or pie. Candy was succeeding in staying ahead of the hatchet man TV talent with her lip smacking short cuts. Not to mention the boost in her catering profile that resulted from the one-biter "Mini." And the higher profit margin.

Candy had scrapped the walls between the kitchen and living room and had converted the area to a nifty four hundred square foot custom-made industrial baker's kitchen. The small guest room, adjacent to the kitchen, was furnished only with a bed. Since her best recipe ideas came to her during the night, keeping a bed a few steps away from the kitchen facilitated effective middle of the night baking tests (sleeping was an enormous waste of time, anyway). The proper bedroom was nothing more than a pack-rat dumping ground for clothing, except for one corner where there was a clearing for a futon and a TV. All in all, the arrangement worked well for her, utilizing every inch of useable space.

Even with the custom design and all the extra counter tops, the L-shaped kitchen was messy and jumbled with commercial equipment: mixers, blenders, food processors, pastry bags, baking sheets, and baking racks. Sacred shelving space was chock-full of strikingly unusual flours and exotic looking scales from big and bulky to ultra-sleek.

Candy baked with a mad passion. She believed there was no kitchen in the world that could compare with hers. She designed it specifically for her particular needs. It was so perfect. That is, as long as the health and building departments knew nothing of it (there were those darn vents that never worked quite right). They would shut her down faster than a sinking soufflé. The mere mention of a city department to Candy was not a good idea. Anxiety and terror would take over, as she knew she could never beat city hall. She would have to convert her apartment back to its original state and get walloped with a five-figure fine. Then she would have to move to an expensive, yet unremarkable commercial location with out-of-date equipment that would wreck her output and plunder her profit. There was no way in hell she would ever let that happen.

Candy turned on the vintage white radio. It was the top of the hour and there was another breaking story about the alarming rise of date rape in the area, along with a warning for women not to go home with men they've just met, then it was onto a commercial break for *Viagra*.

She leaned against the alternately dull and scratched stainless steel counter and crossed her arms while she thought about what to whip up for dinner. She decided on three dishes, all containing chocolate. She figured Emily to be the high-strung, moody type, so what could be better for one's mood storms than chocolate in large quantities.

"I've been up all night working, in metric," Candy mimicked that uppity Emily as she tamped down chocolate crumbs into a spring-form pan. She snickered as she measured and chopped, mixed and folded, blended and baked. What? Did Emily think working in metric was something Candy would be impressed by? After all, every one of Candy's recipes was in metric. Bopping along with the country and western station, she lit a cigarette. She placed the quivering chocolate cheesecake inside the oven, and started the molten chocolate bomb. Stupid bitch, she thought of Emily, with her uptight ass and stuck-up attitude, no wonder she couldn't keep her man. And all I did was try to be welcoming and she thinks she can slam her door in my face. We'll just see about that, Candy thought, as she grabbed her stepladder in order to fetch her spinning cake stand that sat on a shelf just out of her reach.

Emily had made some progress, but couldn't see straight. It was hopeless. She had to rest her eyes, stretch her legs and just get out.

Emily smiled at the phone. She would call Linda Sterling to see if she were free for lunch. Linda always made her feel better. It had been a couple of weeks and Emily owed her a phone call, but Linda knew that Emily needed her space right now and would let things like an unreturned phone call slide.

"Linda, Em. What's going on?"

"I just turned in the first draft of my manuscript so I am a free woman for a few days. What's been going on with you?"

"Working, moving out, working more, feeling sorry for myself, obsessing over Michael. And in my spare time, trying to start over. All this at my age," Emily said.

"You're ready to emerge?"

"Yes, but it's not easy. How about lunch? I'll tell you all about it," Emily said with a wave of sarcasm wrapping around her words.

"Broadway Deli at one. That easy enough? And you must tell me everything about you and Michael. I do mean everything," Linda said.

"You'll be bored," Emily said.

"Enquiring minds are never bored," Linda said with a laugh as she hung up.

She checked her watch and it read eleven-thirty. She went to her dressing room and sat at the make up table. She deftly twisted and pinned her hair into a sloppy ponytail bun, which highlighted her looks, lessening the frump factor. Pleased at the easy result— *it's a start*— she analyzed her reflection in the mirror and decided it was a day for some serious camouflaging. Fortunately, the tabletop was replete with every type of concealer imaginable. She chose the one formulated for dark circles and applied it seamlessly. Sparkle returned to her brown eyes.

The Broadway Deli was packed and a good energy hung in the air. Emily was five minutes early so she took a seat at the bar and ordered an espresso. Across from her, and in earshot, was a group of five young women, all with tight, petite-cheerleader bodies, and although heavily made-up, they were all gorgeous. They seemed to be fussing over one of the girl's wedding albums, pointing at photos and telling each other how beautiful they looked. One of the girls, pleasingly busty in a tight sweater, asked the others if they thought she should get a boob job.

"Oh, yes, do it! You'll be so happy," another cheerleader look-alike said.

"Your boyfriends will love it," said another.

"I had mine done just for the wedding and my husband is so proud that he shows naked pictures of me to all his friends now," the wedding album girl confidently added.

"Learn anything?" Linda Sterling asked as she and her innate sense of cool came up behind Emily.

"You would not believe this conversation," Emily said.

Linda glanced at the cheerleaders. "Oh yes I would."

The hostess came over to them with menus. "Your booth is ready."

"I'm hungry, let's get a move on," Linda said to Emily, who seemed loath to move from her seat.

"Women like that have it all," Emily mumbled, feeling low again as she pushed herself away from the bar.

"Forget about them. They're as depressed as you are, except they don't have the brains to figure it out," Linda said. The hostess didn't even wait for them to sit before literally throwing their menus on the table because, just then, an actor, with a recurring role on Entourage had walked in. The hostess having her priorities in order, made a beeline to gush over him.

"Don't you just love life in L.A? Pushed aside for some boring cable actor," Emily said as they watched the hostess dote.

"He's not so boring. That guy was on TMZ last night— in a drunken brawl with some Kennedy kids," Linda said as they seated themselves.

No sooner had they sat down a basket of bread was placed on the table. The overly efficient server had arrived to take their order.

"We need another minute," Linda said, shooing her away. The server disappeared as quickly as she had appeared.

"Great, now we'll never get her back," Emily said.

Linda looked Emily in the eye. "So, talk to me. How's your life?" She grabbed a piece of bread and stuffed it in her mouth. "And I don't care about the crossword."

"I'm moving through my emotions. What keeps me up at night is I keep thinking that I want Michael back. But there's no way in hell I could be married to him again. I don't even want to be friends because I can't handle it. I wish I could put the thought of him out of my brain for good. I thought I knew what my heart wanted in getting the divorce. I am trying my best to bury him— bury us. I know I just have to ride it out."

"I'm sorry. You need to cleanse your emotions and that takes time. Two years. Even if you are the one who wanted it."

"That's too long," Emily said.

"You don't have a choice. You two just wanted completely different things. You both gave it a good shot. It was a mistake from the beginning. What I mean is, you two started out as if it were the end," Linda said.

"I miss the intimacy. The bond between us..." Emily said, her voice breaking, unable to finish her sentence.

"I know," Linda said.

"But he just couldn't let me be. Always picking on me. Closing me in. I felt like he was always hammering nails in around me, as if I were in a box. I had no room to breathe. He wanted to control every pore on my body—"

"Honey I want the heart, I want the soul, I want control, right now," Linda sang.

"It sounds great in a song, but in reality no one can live like that," Emily said. "There must be a better way."

"Let's figure it out, bottle it and sell it," Linda said.

"Maybe you've got something there. Anyway, at least I'm busy," Emily said, changing topics. "I went after some luxury clients during my down time and a big project may result from it. I'm only proposing it, but I have a feeling I'll land the thing, so I'll need to pull together a new team right away.

"It's a huge fee! But, I have to be honest; I'm prostituting myself. The client is a maniac and a despicable little shit," Emily said.

"We all have to pick our poison," Linda said.

"Well this poison does take my mind off of Michael. And I must admit, I enjoy my solitude."

"Don't say that to too many people. Solitude is not deemed normal to most. A social life is a good thing to have. I'm sensing a mental deterioration in you and I don't like it," Linda said. With a mouthful of bread she added, "You should go see Chris Rouge, my yoga teacher."

"Chris Rouge? What kind of name is that?"

"It doesn't matter. Just book him for an hour. It will be so good for your spirits. Here's his number," Linda said as she wrote 310-555-6900. The server finally returned to take their order, only after she had spent an inordinate amount of time reading the entire menu to the cable star, who then decided he didn't want anything after all, and left.

After they finished lunch, they took a stroll on the Third Street Promenade. It was crowded for midday and they constantly had to dodge other pedestrians, dogs and homeless people. They stopped when they got to a silver-painted acrobat with no hands and no feet, who was doing some amazing contortion act.

"This is too bizarre. See, your life isn't so bad," Linda said as they walked away.

Just as they were squeezing through an area packed with knots of people watching a young, Asian-American version of Jimi Hendrix, two large men who looked very similar to each other, were abominably bullying their way through the crowd, pushing people, knocking an old lady down and scaring small children. The two big men may have been twins. Maybe they were just brothers, or friends who styled themselves alike. As the men pushed their way through the people, one of them stepped on Emily's toe and elbowed her in the ribs at the same time. "Watch it," she yelled, as the *sasquatches* disappeared into the multi-ethnic horde.

"Apes," Linda Sterling said as she flipped them the bird.

"They're nothing compared to my new neighbor," Emily said as she rubbed her toe.

FOUR

EMILY SLICED HER PALM with the X-ACTO knife. Candy's loud knock had caught her off guard while she was cutting the white border off a photo for the presentation. Blood squirted everywhere, but miraculously just missed the intensely labored-over, precisely laid-out, almost-finished material board, and continued to spurt on anything within arm's length. The knocking was boisterous and unsettling, and as she looked toward the front door she noticed the clock said 7:30. Already in disarray from cutting herself, she remembered Candy's message from earlier that day. "This better be good," she said to herself, disgusted and bloody, as she went to answer the door. The pounding continued loudly and Emily had no doubt that anyone else's knuckles would have been bruised by now.

"Stop it, I'm coming," she yelled, competing with the noise. As she opened the door, there was Candy, all smiles, wearing an ugly black and white jagged striped shirt and holding a couple of strikingly bedecked picnic baskets. Emily turned and ran into the bathroom to tend to her wound, yelling to Candy, "Come in and set up where you can. I cut myself."

"Let me help. I know just how to fix such a thing. I'm always cutting and burning myself in the kitchen," Candy said. She put down the baskets on Emily's finished presentation boards and ran after her into the bathroom. Grabbing Emily's hand, she pulled it up to her face where she examined it, all the while with a peculiar expression.

"I can take care of it, really," Emily said, not believing that Candy could do something about a cut that she couldn't.

"Really, yourself! I have some ointment upstairs that will make it feel better and prevent any infection. Here now, run it under cold water and I'll be right back," Candy said, as she turned on the tap and stuck Emily's hand in the running water.

"Ow, this is hot!" Emily yelled out, but all she heard from Candy was very loud, clunky footsteps running out and up the stairs.

Minutes later Candy returned with some concoction she had in an unlabeled jar. "This will clean it up and start the healing process a.s.a.p," she said as she reached for Emily's palm.

"What is in that, exactly?"

"Exactly? I don't know. Maybe, Tea Tree oil and some other things. But I do know it works! Come on. Don't be stupid. That's a nasty gash you got there."

Reluctantly, Emily handed over her palm. After all, what's the worst that could happen? Candy slathered and massaged the grainy cream into the cut. For a moment some relief radiated into her hand. Whatever was in that cream it sure worked fast. Emily realized she had judged Candy too quickly. She let out a deep breath as the potion soothed her and felt awful for not trusting Candy. But suddenly, her face was on fire with a mean heat and she couldn't feel her hand at all. The numbness began traveling up her arm.

"Something's wrong! I can't feel my hand or my arm!" Emily was panicking now.

"Well, it's got to feel better than before," Candy said snottily as she went over to unpack the dinner. Once she had set the baskets aside, Emily's jaw dropped as she noticed that there were large grease marks from the footprint of the baskets on the presentation boards— the very same boards that she had to show the clients in less than twelve hours.

"My presentation boards!" Emily shrieked.

"Well they *are* taking up the whole table top. I can't put my beautiful baskets on the floor. That would be unsanitary," Candy said, as she grabbed a couple of paper plates and *Frisbee*-tossed them on to the table, where one landed between a camera and the blood tinged X-ACTO knife.

Emily's blood began to boil and she became light-headed. As her vision blurred to a hazy black she lost her balance. She hit the ground, but not before she bashed her head on the corner of the table.

When she came to, the living room was thick with cigarette smoke and Candy, entombed in a dream world stupor, was snoring on the sofa, a burned-down cigarette between her fingers. There was a half-eaten chocolate cheesecake on the coffee table, on the floor a stepped-on chocolate bomb and a trail of chocolate footprints, and something three-dimensional smeared on the wall behind the sofa, which also appeared to be made of chocolate.

Severely allergic to cigarette smoke, and with her head pounding, Emily opened the front door and stood outside for a minute to clear her lungs. Back inside she opened a couple of windows. She noticed that the feeling in her hand had returned, and that the cut was healing nicely. Her first instinct was to grab her camera and take a few shots of Candy and the chocolate mess; for what purpose, she didn't exactly know. It just felt like the right thing to do.

Candy woke up to a flash in her eyes and Emily wheezing. The clock said two a.m. She fumbled for a cig, but was all out. "I guess I must have smoked them all. I came down here with a whole pack!" she said, still groggy.

Completely agitated again, Emily hissed, "Go home, I have to re-do my work thanks to you. I can't fucking believe it. Look what you've done to my living room—"

"Your eyes are really puffy," Candy said.

"From your fucking cigarettes! Just leave me alone." She walked over to the open front door and stood there. "Out. Now."

"Hey, I have a great cream for red, puffy eyes—"

Emily ran at Candy, grabbed her by both arms, dragged her out the door and then kicked her square in the ass, which sent Candy to the ground face first. Emily stormed back inside to grab the picnic baskets, which she threw at Candy's head and then slammed the door shut.

"Now Emily, don't be ungrateful," Candy whispered to the night as she regained her footing and gathered up her baskets.

FIVE

EMILY POPPED AN *Adderall* and chased it with a *Red Bull*. She needed to be in tunnel focus mode as rescheduling the presentation wasn't an option because the client was getting more than one proposal. There was no way in hell she would lose this one— especially because of that woman upstairs.

Getting down to business, as the pill kicked in, Emily worked through the next few hours seamlessly in monomania. She had decided to leave the mess in the living room; she would clean it up later. Focusing with precision on the presentation boards, each dedicated to one element of the project, the previous evening a distant blur, the finish line was in sight. Two more hours, she figured, then she could take a shower, and maybe even have time for coffee. She stood up and stretched, took a step back from the boards, and knew instantly that the compositional charm of the penis-shaped lobby needed more prominence.

While enlarging the penis lobby, she thought she heard a muffled, vaguely sexual, moaning. Emily muted the sound on the TV, rendering the early morning infomercial silent. Sure enough, the sound was coming from upstairs through the heat vent, with the physical thrusts resonating through the ceiling. The moans graduated into dirty talking and then into dirty yelling. As unbelievable as it seemed, there was no mistaking that Candy was having the fuck of her life right above Emily's head. Even more unbelievable to Emily, was that someone was brave enough to sleep with Candy Jones.

Emily grabbed a baseball bat she kept nearby for self defense and, with full force, whacked the ceiling. "You asshole, shut up," she screamed.

Not only did the fucking noise increase now, making matters worse, thumping and crashing sounds underscored it. Emily, stress hormone levels spiked and wound up tight on the brain steroid, knew she had to concentrate on finishing her project. A chunk of plaster fell from the ceiling and bounced off her head right onto her work, denting one of the foam core boards. She cringed and told herself it was all a minor inconvenience, nothing more. She protectively eyed all her presentation boards, and began to carefully move them aside along with various scraps of literature and fabrics, the glue gun and the blood and debris-sticky utility knife. She had to shield her work from any more falling rubble.

The sounds of pleasure continued, reverberating through the heat vent, rattling the metal, and thus rattling Emily. This wasn't a minor inconvenience anymore. With the bat still in arm's reach, and without another thought, she ran outside and into the dead of night.

The vast darkness was ripped wide open, ruptured with churning flashes that took turns coloring the black sky and by the accompanying explosion of sirens wailing full throttle. A couple of hook and ladder fire trucks had taken the corner way too fast. The first rear tiller driver was now frantically regaining traction, as was the second truck, about three seconds behind him. The trucks rumbled and roared up the street just as she bounded over the driveway hedge, *Louisville Slugger* in hand, and went for Candy's windshield. It didn't take much for the glass to promptly shatter, while the ground trembled from the aftershock of the speeding red machines.

Emily exhaled, felt the tension evaporate from her shoulders and started back to her place with a skip in her step. But her feeling of vindication lasted only a fleeting moment, because just as the sky retrogressed to unbroken black, she realized that she had locked herself out.

As Candy peered through the blinds into the yard she witnessed Emily's tantrum taking over her body: contorting and writhing, twisting and turning. Candy had seen some bizarre things in her life. She would have been more concerned if Emily hadn't been so horrible by shoving her and kicking her earlier that day. Her new neighbor was certainly a hothead. Candy walked back to bed, unplugged the magic wand and went to sleep.

SIX

THE ABYSMAL ALL-NIGHTER was reflected not only in her clumsy presentation that morning, but also in her appearance. The morning had not allowed for make up. She never found her hairbrush. Her blouse was stained. Her skirt was—well, wrong.

Emily saw the previous design team leave. From every angle they appeared to be a unified machine of perfection. By-the-book corporate dress code clothes bore no wrinkles. Not one team member slouched. They even seemed to all be the same height and weight. Seven people operating as one against her one-person team. She knew they had given a kick-ass presentation, because that's what those kinds of teams do, nothing less. She wondered how she could even compete with their proposal, let alone their stellar physical presence. They would be a hard act to follow. She had deluded herself in thinking she could get this project.

The client, the impeccably dressed and over-groomed Dar Aroubian, was seated in a plush, high backed chair at the large, exceedingly ornate conference table waiting for Emily to wow him with her ideas for his Beverly Hills erotic art gallery and gift shop. They had met two months ago to review the preliminary plans, but now he acted like he had never seen Emily before. Upon him laying eyes on her, he was neither impressed nor amused.

He gave her the visual once over, his brow furrowing as he attempted to understand her curious choice of hairstyle. Then he stared off into oblivion.

Emily stood to the left of the presentation screen and skill-fully pulled her mental self together. After the night she had, she wasn't about to look back. From here on out she was only going forward. She rolled her shoulders back, puffed out her chest, inflated her ego, swung one leg forward (which got his attention because the gesture allowed a toned thigh to peek through the inappropriately high slit in her unsuitably snug skirt), placed her hand on her hip and looked him dead in the eye.

"Your gallery is going to transport people on an erotic journey. What better way to explore this passage (she emphasized pas-sage) than by a deconstruction and an incorporation of the word sensual—"

"Sexual, not sensual," Dar interrupted. He had a lisp.

This broke her concentration. Clients would often interrupt during presentations, but today she was ripe for breaking focus, due to that fucking Candy. Additionally, she was coming down from the *Adderall* marathon, so she was part spacey, part giddy. She really hoped she wouldn't crack a smile at his impediment.

"Sensual is more appealing to a much broader market," Emily riffed, hoping he wouldn't take it as disrespect or contradiction. This was a man who was used to everyone saying yes to him.

"The kinder, gentler version, if you will—"

"I want the X. Sensual doesn't have an X. The X expands my market to every corner of the world. X-rated, XXX, X marks the spot. It's Se-X-ual. That's what I want. If my patrons include mother's milk freaks and tranny-porn fetishists, so be it." Dar said as he slammed his hand on the table.

"I will now explain my concept in relation to the design," Emily said, choosing to disregard Dar's outburst. These clients think they know everything, she thought. Sometimes, it was just the art of the banter and nothing more, or the art of the chutz-pah in this case. They just had to throw some weight around. She was well acquainted with the type. She wanted to roll her eyes but didn't. As edgy as she was, remaining professional was her only option if she wanted to nail the project. He was, after all, considering hiring her for her expertise. And, he was paying a magnificent fee.

The floor plan presentation would be done via PowerPoint on the big screen. In addition there were two material boards with fabrics and flooring materials for touching and testing, and two more boards with custom developed color and finish samples set up on low easels on the conference table.

Emily continued with her version of the underlying theme for the gallery.

"S," she said, as a large swirling S came up on the screen, "is for Sappho, the greatest of early Greek erotic poets. The lyrical quality of poetry will be represented in metaphor throughout the space in the open flow and subtle transitions."

"E is for the Enlightenment," she said, as a scrolling E materialized, "which represents the thinkers of natural virtue and honesty in art in the way the niches will be featured, thus capturing the specific emotion that the artist has intended for the viewer.

"N is for Neo-Romanticism, which references an attitude of thought that allows itself to show in surprising ways." Emily turned around to see if Dar was engaged. She noticed him yawning. She tried not to react to his disinterest and kept going without loosing a beat.

"The second S is for—"

"I get it, let's cut to the design," Dar said dismissively, looking at his watch, wondering where he would have lunch today. She figured she had lost him and feared the project outcome for the worst. He would not look at her. Her posture slumped and she regretted not paying more attention to her appearance this morning. As she began to twist her hair on the back of her head into a smart knot, she took the liberty of overruling his authority.

"We must preserve the literary d.n.a. of these themes or the art's complexity will be nothing more than smut one can view through a peep hole," Emily said, praying she wasn't pushing it with him. At the same time, she couldn't find enough of her hair to make a knot— something she could do with her eyes closed. *Why can't I—*

"I'm not an bloody idiot. My time is valuable. Show me the gallery now," Dar demanded, pulling rank.

Emily stopped multi-thinking and fast-forwarded to the image of the floor plan. The phallic-shaped lobby was so over-the-top that there was no way anyone could mistake it for anything else. The gallery niches were in the shape of breasts with protruding nipples, and the front entry doors bore a strong resemblance to a shapely rear end. And that was just the beginning.

On seeing this, Dar shot out of his chair and virtually ran over to the screen. At five feet five inches in height, lifts included, he was face to face with the lobby. He stared at it and then peered closely at the entry doors and niches. He began passing his hands over the spaces, seemingly caressing the images. She hadn't a clue what was in his head. He was so hard to read, just like Michael.

This was the first time Emily saw the whole floor plan in this large screen format. She was in disbelief. How could she have done that? What was she thinking? Was she out of her mind? Dar turned around to face her. He was standing in the middle of the screen, so the floor plan was now over his body, making him part of the presentation.

"I like it. It's tasteful. It's classy. Enormously sexy curves and fantastically straight, hard, lines— two points of view that fit perfect together. These are not bowdlerized references like those other proposals; these are grand-scale, human anatomy obvious and audaciously original. And give me that peep-hole you mentioned— that will be our big draw. This is better than I could have imagined. Let's go ahead, I don't want to waste any more time. Ask my business manager, Andrea, for whatever you need to get started."

That was the last thing Emily expected to hear. All that ran through her mind was that now she would have to build out this atrocity. She couldn't find the right words. She was speechless.

"Two things," Dar added as he stared at the stain on her blouse, "Your *sensual* concept is too bland. Lose the *n* and the second *s* and replace it with *x*. End of story. That's the deal."

"The other?" Emily asked, barely audible.

"The colors are boring and distasteful. I hate them."

"But these colors are sophisticated and contemporary. And that is an amazing gray," Emily said pointing to the understated and warm tone on the board that she had mixed herself.

"The palette is to be..." Dar said gleefully arrogant, tuning her and her gloomy hues out as he looked around for an inspiration, his eyes stopping on his reflection in the wall mounted TV, "the color of my tie."

He removed his tie and tossed it on the custom color board. She picked it up and examined it closely.

"But it's...it's..." she said shaking her head as she looked up to his back as he zipped out the door. She ran after him, but he was gone.

"Purple!" she yelled to an empty hall.

SEVEN

EMILY HAD TAKEN UP LINDA STERLING on her offer to have a private yoga session with Chris Rouge. What she really needed was to get some shut-eye, but she was in that twilight zone headspace and knew she wouldn't be able to sleep; she was too wired. She had just enough time to get home, move some boxes out of the way and clear an area to practice yoga. Chris was due at two p.m.

As she pulled up to the loft, Candy's car was still at the far end of the driveway, windshield still smashed out. She noticed that the car was very dusty, but didn't think twice about it— Candy was a pig. Deep inside, Emily hoped the whole situation with her neighbor would resolve itself. Maybe, after all, they had just gotten off on the wrong foot. She really didn't want to have to move again.

Emily's place was a disaster. She had worked up to the last minute possible, then packed everything and left for Dar Aroubian's office. She eyed the trash heap like it was the enemy and considered her best line of attack. Foam board remnants, various unspecified splinters, shreds of fabric and Velcro fragments were strewn all over.

The perfectionist Emily of yore would have been embarrassingly distraught by this wreckage. But the modernized Emily, no longer beholden to her penchant for all things perfect, could now transcend this moment and not allow something as trifle as an epic mess to obsessively occupy her mental self. She would declare war on this battlefield of garbage another time.

She looked around for a clearing. The living room was a packed parking lot of big boxes. Furniture jammed and bottlenecked most usable space, not to mention the area remained unchanged from the chocolate fiasco. She followed the revolting dessert skid marks from the table, to the floor and up the wall where her eyes locked on the vertical smear, in particular on the foreign substance enmeshed within. She touched the back of her head and the math was obvious. Her missing tresses were, up until now, the unidentifiable medium in chocolate bas-relief. She knotted up inside. This was pure sickness on Candy's part. Something was dreadfully wrong with that woman upstairs.

After doing a speedy feathery fix on her locks with the utility knife and precision handling, she steered her way into the only right-brained room in the place, the tranquil sanctuary of her bedroom— courtesy of left-brained master planning. She would test drive it's potential with Chris. The possibility being that this inside space would help her effortlessly embrace her outside miseries and accept the gap in her heart.

She was about to slide the bed over to the wall when she heard a gentle knock at the door, the door opening, and a man's voice asking for her.

"In here," she yelled, as she came out of the bedroom. She saw his silhouette in the open door frame with the sunlight behind him. She perked up at this sight— *enchanté what can I say*— and walked over to him and extended her hand.

"I'm Emily. Nice to meet you."

"I'm Chris. I've heard a lot about you from Linda." He had an unbelievable smile, reminding her of the sun-tanned weatherman on the local television news.

"I think the bedroom is the best place for us to do our thing, given all this mess," Emily said.

"Okay," he said.

She smiled back to him like she couldn't help it. She felt so relaxed, so right, in his presence. They headed for the bedroom. He went over to the window and closed the drapes. He pulled a couple of scented candles out of his bag and lit them. They glowed softly on the bedside table.

"Let's move the bed over," she said. "We'll have more room that way."

"No, it's fine the way it is. We can work on top of the bed. I prefer if you remove your clothes, but only if you are comfortable."

Emily had never heard of doing yoga on a bed before, let alone naked. She only agreed to it because she had never seen a more beautiful man. Not even Michael.

"Lay on your back with your arms out to the side, palms up. Close your eyes. You are one with the bed beneath you." Emily felt the bed move as he climbed up and positioned himself next to her. "Allow yourself to forget about your day. Forget about outside distractions." His voice was almost a whisper. "Concentrate on your breathing. Bring your breath to your throat. It will sound like the wind. Extend your inhale to be as deep as your exhale."

Emily entered into an ethereal space at that moment as the recent chaos and upheaval vanished from her consciousness. Chris continued his instruction ever so softly and she thought for a moment he was caressing her ears. Whatever he was doing to her, she didn't care. It was working. She was in a state of bliss.

Then the car chase happened. Loud, screeching tires and crashing and slamming sounds, with even louder music. It must have been many cars, chasing and racing. There was a rhythm to it. It would last about fifteen seconds, then there would be quiet, then it would happen again, the exact same sounds. Then Emily got it. It wasn't coming from the street, but from above.

She opened her eyes and saw Chris looking at the ceiling. The noise was obscene, but Chris just gave her that weatherman smile and shrugged his shoulders. "Maybe we should relocate. One must transcend life's distractions. Breathe deep," he said, leaning his head back.

Emily's blood pressure spiked, her blissful state crashed. She couldn't get Candy's face out of her mind. "We'll do this another time. I mean it." She wasn't going to blow her chances with Chris;

she would re-schedule. "I'll walk you out," she said, grabbing an old dress shirt of Michael's from the wall hook. She buried her face in it and breathed in the musky infused threads before she slipped it on.

He insisted she keep the candles burning in order to release the healing fragrance to keep her calm. He kissed her on the cheek, they took deep breaths and exhaled together and he kissed her again on the other cheek. Then she watched as he departed on his bicycle.

The car chase noise penetrated the entire first floor of the loft, and boomed into the yard. Emily finished the last of the deep breaths, grabbed her wallet and keys then went upstairs. Candy's door was wide open so she went inside. The noise was still blaring, even louder now as she was closer to the source. She was amazed to see an industrial baker's kitchen right here in her building. It was a magnificent vision in stainless steel. She followed the cigarette smoke and noise to an area that wasn't clad in steel. There, in a small room, with clothes piled six feet high, sat Candy Jones on a mystery-stained futon that was propped up on one side by a sturdy steel baking pan. Next to it, was a towering stack of tome-size, dog-eared cookbooks crowned with a tray on top. Emily had seen that cheap end-table trick on the DIY sites for years. Candy had an intense look in her eyes, a remote control in her hand and was replaying over and over the famous car chase from *Bullitt*.

"Candy!" Emily yelled.

"Here, sit down," Candy yelled back, slapping the futon seat next to her, still staring at the television. She looked up at Emily and seeing the horrible expression on her face, she tossed a threadbare throw over the nasty stains.

"Turn it down!" Emily yelled with her hands covering her ears. "And I'm not putting my ass on that thing!"

"This has been bugging me for years. I've been trying to figure this out," Candy said as she muted the volume, "I swear they used the same scene over and over again for this chase. I've played it over so many times. They think we don't notice things like that. Well I do, and I'm going to do something about it. Look. See, it's the same scene, over and over. I've counted twelve times *Steve McQueen* has gone around this corner, gone past the pink car and skidded." Candy queued the DVD to the scene and then played it. And again. Emily watched. Candy did have a point.

"And what about my hair?" Emily stood in front of the TV and turned her head to show Candy.

"What about it? It was your idea," Candy said, "You wanted me to cut it. I tried to talk you out of it."

"Don't put this back on me!"

"I helped you. You said you wanted an...edgier....look."

"I never would have said *that*," Emily said, throwing her arms down to her sides.

"You just don't remember because you blacked out. I'm on to your behavior." Candy said.

"*My* behavior? What are you saying?"

"No good deed goes unpunished. That's what I'm saying. We need to drop this if we are going to be neighbors. I'll stay out of your hair from now on— get it? Hah! I better get back to my centerpiece," Candy said as she tossed the remote aside. She took out a cigarette from her apron pocket. "You're not the only one around here with deadlines, you know. Hey, how did your meeting go?"

Startled at the about face, she didn't want Candy to know about her business so she turned the topic in order to try to get to know more about this woman. "This is an amazing kitchen. Are you in catering?"

"I'm a pastry chef," Candy said proudly, lighting her cigarette and blowing smoke at Emily, causing Emily to move around the cloud. "I designed this place myself. I didn't need a decorator or designer or consultant or whatever you call yourselves these days. I saved thousands of dollars in decorator fees. Why would I throw away money like that? That's like flushing cash down the toilet."

This wasn't the first time Emily had heard those kinds of comments. Always the pro, she was armed with all kinds of comebacks (most of them civilized) to throw a Do-It-Yourselfer into a tailspin of self doubt. She dug the knife in a bit:

"Good for you! How did you get this kitchen past Building and Safety? Or the Health department?" Emily asked, knowing that industrial kitchens weren't allowed in residential zones. Additionally, the place was loaded with code violations, assaulting her trained eye wherever she looked.

Candy's body language changed. "Oh I have all my licenses." She looked at her watch. "Uh, I really have to get back to work," she said as she flashed a hangdog smile at Emily.

Emily noticed something human and vulnerable about Candy right then; there was something in her eyes behind those glasses deeper than her obvious imperfection. Emily dropped the mindfuck and decided to take the high road, since it was clear that Candy never would. Maybe, she thought now would be the time to start over.

"We got off on the wrong foot. I'm sorry about your windshield. I'll replace it. I found out how much it cost. Here's three hundred dollars," she said taking some cash from her wallet and placing it in Candy's apron pocket.

"Well, that's doing your research. You know, you really don't have to give me money," Candy said with a genuinely serious look as she took the money from her pocket and counted it. She directed her next exhale away from Emily and then fanned the cloud of smoke to help dissipate it.

"Really, I want to," Emily said with finality, and turned to go back to her place. Despite Candy letting her off the hook, Emily was still troubled by the fact that she had acted so impulsively and inanely in smashing the windshield. She had never behaved like that before.

EIGHT

"**Z**OOM IN CLOSER. Are you getting this?" The larger one, Tino, said to his brother.

"She's not that hot, she looks like a cadaver," Gino said, as he focused on the passed-out woman his brother was fucking.

"Come on, she's having a real good time, look at her," Tino said, as he flopped her lifeless legs around. "She loves it!"

"The one last week was better, at least she grunted," Gino said, trying to be creative as he filmed.

"The redhead?" Tino asked as he pounded away effortlessly on the very wan and tiny woman, who had drool coming from the corner of her mouth.

"Not that one, knucklehead. The one we put up on YouTube, last night. Remember?"

The cheaply furnished apartment had a mattress on the floor, a disintegrating curtain that was partially fallen from the track, and an old metal chair with a flaking vinyl seat. Tino Biscotti rolled off of the frail and abused body.

"Your turn. Give me the camera. I'll show you how to make a movie!"

"And I'll show you how to fuck her like a real man, you faggot," the slightly smaller Gino said to his twelve-minute younger brother. Tino grabbed his brother's face with one hand and yanked it hard down to his eye level.

"Hardy-fucking-har. Next time you talk to me like that you're gonna put on a wig and lacy panties and take her place," Tino said, looking his brother straight in the eye.

"Okay, no big thing, man," Gino said. "It's cool, everything's cool, bro."

NINE

CANDY PICKED UP THE UZI from her baking counter and examined it from all angles. She had acquired it in a parking lot outside the gun show last week at the Glendale Civic Center. She had been looking for inspiration for her next big event— the upcoming *NRA Right to Carry Concealed Weapons* banquet at the *Sportsman Lodge in Studio City*. None of the weapons at the gun show had inspired her. They were all too new and sleek, not to mention overpriced.

Walking to her car, a fat, bald and bearded desert-rat in combat fatigues had flagged her down. He said he needed some fast cash and she could own his gun in return. The deal closer was when he told her she wouldn't even have to register it, as she would if she had bought one inside the show or from a dealer, which would not only save her time, but money (no sales tax). He had told Candy he'd rather give her a good deal than give the pinko government any money, so the transaction worked out nicely for each of them.

She placed the gun back down on the counter. She studied each orifice and every curve. Candy needed to absorb its energy and feel its power before she could begin creating. This parking lot Uzi came from a real anti-government, survivalist, maybe even a domestic terrorist. She liked the grit associated with that and knew it would contribute to a truthful result. She closed her eyes and imagined it (but quadrupled in size and in marzipan) a stunning centerpiece for the dessert table. Surely, everyone would fuss over it. Surely, it would be award winning. Surely, it would propel her to the Food Network or Home Shopping Channel, where she could promote her soon-to-be-finished dessert book.

She lit a cigarette and began tracing the outline of the Uzi onto a piece of cardboard. She would have to make a few mock-ups in order to perfect the scale and detail. Once that was completed, the actual centerpiece would be made. This was an important show for Candy, not just because of the commercial potential, but because the NRA had lots of banquets and were big spenders when it came to food and drink. If they liked her desserts, they might contract her to cater all their local events. She had no alternative but to shine in their eyes. She had already perfected the individual desserts. The tiramisu would be in the shape of the Uzi magazine, and the take-home lollipops for the NRA kids in the shape of the banned Saturday Night Special handgun, wrapped in pastel colored cellophane with blue ribbons for the boys and pretty pink for the girls.

TEN

EARLY THE NEXT MORNING, Emily went out to her *Pilates* class. She had a couple of sessions left on the gift certificate from Linda, and wanted to use them before they expired. Like everything else in her life, the Pilates routine had fallen by the wayside. Determined to keep some kind of schedule, she figured an early session would be a welcome fit right now. Once inside the building, she registered at the sign-in sheet and went into the studio. She claimed one of the five reformers. A young woman followed her in, came toward her and smiled. Clearly the woman wanted to speak with her.

"Tell me, you're THE interior designer?" the woman asked.

"Yes," Emily answered as she studied the woman's face. She was sure she didn't know her.

I'm Alice Robbins. We haven't met before, but I just saw your name on the sign-in sheet. My boss knows you. He is a huge fan of yours. I've left you several messages recently but I haven't heard back. My boss is remodeling and he had me track you down. He doesn't want to work with anyone else. He said 'Get me uh... Emma...Everwood,' " the determined, energetic and cherubic junior executive said, tripping over Emily's name.

"Emily Everheart," Emily said. She eyed the young woman and tried to digest it all. None of this made any sense, but when opportunity knocks, things don't necessarily have to add up. Still, Emily's gut was warning her: something is off here.

"I'd love to speak with your boss about the remodel. You say we know one another?" Emily probed.

"He told me he knows you and to get you on board. I'll set up a meeting and we'll confirm at class tomorrow. You will be here?" Emily nodded. "I'm so thrilled to meet you. It really is an honor," Alice Robbins said.

Emily still couldn't figure out why Alice was pouring on the flattery. It wasn't warranted, even if Alice was scoring a few points for her boss. Just then the instructor came in a yelled at everyone to get on the reformers.

"First position! Everybody! Let's go!" The four women and one man assumed the basic bar posture and began the session on their backs. For one hour, Emily was in another world of sit-bones, belly buttons, elephants and mermaid-twists. They ended the class on the spinal roll-up and roll-down. Emily lay on the reformer for a minute to catch her breath. She watched as the man in the class continued with a few more roll-ups. Mr. Torso must have been a dancer or a tennis player. His form was flawless. His physique was perfect, like one of Dar Aroubian's sculptures. She continued to stare at him working out, enjoying the view.

"See you tomorrow," Alice Robbins said, recapturing Emily's attention. "I really am so happy to have met you!"

Emily decided to lighten up. So she had a fan— big deal. Emily didn't have to be so negative about someone who had nice things to say. Not everyone in the world was an asshole.

It was almost time to meet Linda for breakfast— which was good timing because Emily needed Linda's advice. She had begun mentally mobilizing a design team to help her with executing Dar's gallery, but she was not looking forward to explaining the concept to prospective consultants. She would have to weed out anyone who was a bit conservative or squeamish about being exposed to so much human form. After she finished examining the most recent barrage of one hundred and twenty resumes that flooded her e-mail box, she would set up interviews.

They met for breakfast at Patrick's Roadhouse. Unshaven, baseball-capped, hip-looking men in jeans discussing their *projects* dominated the place. A few waifish, ultra-anorexic young women, still rumpled from their sleep were out on the patio getting blown around by the wind coming off the ocean. Linda was already there, finishing up a conversation on her cell as Emily spotted her in the last apple-green booth.

"Who was that?" Emily asked as she sat down.

"My agent," Linda said.

"I have had my head up my ass for so long, I forgot to ask you what's going on with the book. It's about anti-dating, right?"

"Yes, for us women of a certain age. It's a close-up look at how men rate women by body parts versus how women rate men—"

"JAC?"

"Job, apartment and car? Not our generation. Junk, ass and cash is the new JAC. We're as appalling as the opposite sex is.

"Everything *was* going well. Until now. My agent's telling me I can't refer to every guy as Dick. So I can't talk about it right now. I need to take my mind off of it, so let's talk about you. Please."

After telling Linda all about landing the gallery project and starting her interviews, she confided, "I'm not quite sure how to characterize the project to the new team. I've given it a lot of thought and I'm stumped."

"That's your own hang-up. People love porn— hey, can we get a menu?" Linda yelled to no one in particular. "It's in most people's homes. If kids and congressmen are sexting, then why can't you have a porno project," Linda pointed out. "If you're embarrassed about it, get over it. I'm telling you, no one will turn you down. In fact, they'll probably offer to work on it for free."

Emily mused out loud, "An erotic gallery and pleasure shop?"

"Call it whatever makes you comfortable. As I said before, you won't have a problem assembling a crew. Now, how was Chris?"

"That's another story," Emily softened as she thought about it, "I was surprisingly comfortable with him. I think I would have slept with him if it weren't for my upstairs neighbor."

"What happened? Did she get to him first?" Linda asked, looking alarmed.

"No, well, not like you're thinking. I do want to see him again. I do need some male touch. At the moment he's my fantasy," Emily said as she picked the cantaloupe out of her fruit salad.

Linda reached over with her fork and transferred the unwanted melon to her plate. "I'm sure he'd love to hear from you. You should get to know him. But do know he won't leave his wife. He's giving her some space after squeezing out so many kids for him. The last one nearly split her in two. I don't think she wants sex ever again— can't really blame her. So she's given him the all clear to have affairs— affairs of the flesh, not of the heart. He's really stepped up his fatherhood. I'd say he's over-actively engaged in his kids' lives," Linda said.

"Sounds like a mostly rock-solid guy. I think I can handle that. I'm not ready for a traditional relationship anyway. I'm still in love with Michael. Not a day goes by that I don't think about him. I have to start not loving him," Emily confessed. She took a sip of water and composed herself. "About Chris— he rides a bike. What's the deal with that?"

"Some temporary freedom, I'd imagine, from his home life," Linda said.

"Got it. I thought maybe he was poor," Emily said, her nose crinkled.

"He does okay. He owns his own yoga studio and the building it's in. I can assure you that riding that bike doesn't affect anything he can do, in case you were concerned," Linda said, as she sat back with a confident look.

"You've tried him on for size?" Emily asked.

"He threw me a mercy once. I don't think I'm his type. I tried to follow up, but he never pursued me after that. This way I can live vicariously though you," Linda said.

ELEVEN

EMILY GOT THERE SEVERAL MINUTES EARLY to meditate before the others arrived. She had an intense day ahead of her with the interviews. She lay in *savasana* position on the reformer. In too short a time, she began to hear the other members coming into the studio, but managed to keep them out of her consciousness for now. She needed more chill time. Emily kept her eyes shut and tried to tune the noise out.

But now an aggressive footfall was coming toward her— thumpity-thump— *Sigerson Morrison* designed, wedge-heeled footsteps vibrating the studio floor. The footsteps circled Emily's reformer three times.

"You lied to me. You're not Editha Eggars. My boss says he doesn't know you. He says he has never even heard of you," a reproachful Alice Robbins seethed. Emily opened her eyes. Alice was red-faced and looked as if she had been up all night crying. She circled the reformer one more time and then changed directions.

"My boss screamed at me and called me a dumb cunt. I may have lost my job over this. Everyone at the company is laughing at me behind my back. And to my face. Not only that, my boss posted it on his Facebook wall and sent out a Tweet. The whole world knows what a looser I am! I'm fucked! My career is fucked! And all because of you!" Alice said, as she looked Emily square in the eye and then spat on her. Alice stormed out of the studio, hyperventilating and mumbling gibberish. Just twenty-four hours ago

Emily had a fervent admirer fawning over her. What a difference a day makes.

I should have listened to my gut, Emily thought as she wiped the spit off of her face.

"You poor thing. I used to be in the service business myself. I know how dreadful it can be," a low, throaty voice said from the reformer to her right.

"Easy come, easy go," Emily said, devaluing the startling encounter.

"I couldn't help overhear. You are a designer? I'm having quite the time finding someone to design a wine cellar. The proposals I've received are...well, bland at best and even worse, all the same.

"Lots of sameness out there these days. Bad news is it's become acceptable. But the good news is, not from me," Emily said.

"Sameness has never been and will never be in my vocabulary. Is it possible that you can be of some help?"

Emily looked at the woman. She had the whitest hair Emily had ever seen. She wore it long and down, parted asymmetrically, coquettishly covering one emotionless eye. The snow white cascade fell behind her opposite ear, trailed down and embraced her graceful Audrey Hepburn neck, which lead one's eyes down to an flattened outline of cleavage, mummy-wrapped in a white cashmere band that emphasized her lack of curves. She appeared west-side civilized and brimming of taste. Nothing about her said sameness. Everything about her said money.

"You have to promise you won't spit on me," Emily said.

"I think I can honor that. I'm Viv Wyntor," the chic woman said as she held out her hand.

I'm Emily Everheart," Emily said. If this woman was from the Forbes 400 Wyntor family, no problem— she could spit in her face. There were a few of them in Santa Monica. "Yes, I can help you with your wine cellar."

"Excellent. This is my last class here. I gave it my all, but it's not working out. I can't practice naturally here. I'll have to find another studio or build my own. Anyway. I'm digressing. You can talk to Ralph about the wine cellar. He's the man over there hold-ing my *Birkin* and Mr. T," Viv Wyntor said as she pointed to the front waiting area. Emily's eye's followed. Ralph looked bored to tears— not in the way a husband would (mentally on another planet), but in the way a butler would (adeptly domesticated). There was a tiny Chinese Crested dog in his lap. The dog was hairless with the exception a white Mohawk.

"First position, people!" the instructor yelled as she walked over to them. "We have a no-show," she said as she looked at the empty reformer where Alice Robbins would have been. "Does Ralph want a workout this morning?" the instructor asked Viv Wyntor.

"Why, that would be inappropriate. You are aware that he is The Help and he's working right now," Viv Wyntor said quite seriously, as if the whole world should know such protocol.

Back at the office, Emily was halfway through the interviews. She had narrowed the field to five, including a with-it, on-the-ball young Scientologist designer named Chloe who told her she could bring in the Scientology-superstar-and-agent crowd if Emily would sign up to take a few courses. Emily was tempted, but decided that route wasn't for her.

Emily liked Cookie Jennings, who had taken the interview reluctantly as she was pretty sure she wanted to work for herself. So when she declined the offer, Emily was disappointed, as she certain the girl had a lot of talent and would have been an appro-priate addition to the staff.

At the end of the interviews, she had her three hires. One was a recent graduate with phenomenal skills, but with little field and office work. Emily knew that little experience could be good news as well as bad. There would be no stupid habits to break; however, the downside was mistakes would be made in her company name.

But you always need to have at least one person in the office to do the tasks no one else wants to do and Kimiko Arada was thrilled with the idea that she would be able to utilize her skills on this very exciting Beverly Hills Art Gallery of international renown. Kimiko was also looking forward to starting up the e-design department for Emily, something which Emily had no inclination to do herself.

Then there was Beth. Beth Konisberg was a lot like Emily, but fifteen years younger. She boasted a nice resume, and had worked for many designers— many of whom Emily knew— but all for short periods of time. That wasn't so unusual in this business as firms often assemble and disassemble staff as their project load requires, and young designers want to try as many different disciplines as possible before committing to one. Beth was clearly anal about organization, and that suited Emily just fine, since she recently abandoned that skill and needed someone who had it and knew how to implement it. Before Emily discussed the gallery with her, she had asked Beth what kind of space she could see herself designing in the future. Beth had replied with much enthusiasm, "An aphrodisiac-themed restaurant would be really cool," and went into detail on what everything would look, taste, smell and feel like. Beth also admired all the over-the-top and state-of-the-art design that was going on in Las Vegas. A good fit, indeed.

The last hire was Darren Gregson. Energetic, upbeat, smart, educated and experienced, multi-talented and a plus to any firm when that certain spoiled client wants the male designer experience. Emily had lost out on more than one Big Client because she didn't have a guy on her team. Additionally, because of his nurturing nature, he could dote on Emily and, while she didn't require that, some days it would be really helpful and just plain nice. "I can tell you all about the male form and every angle it must be viewed from," he had replied quite seriously when she told him about the Project Dar. "We can compare notes if you wish."

She knew a keeper when she saw one. "Name your price," Emily said.

◈

That evening, Emily removed the ignition key from her key ring and handed it to the valet. Like he cared. Her ten-year old Nissan had been her second office and had fabric samples and flooring boards littered about ad nauseam style. The car was dirty and had dings upon dents on the rear bumper— courtesy of the narrow streets of a recent project for a reality TV show producer in the Hollywood Hills, where one had the space of a postage stamp to turn around in.

The valet took off with her car in reverse at a swift clip and backed it into the parking lot. He ran back to fetch the next car, a brand new Range Rover that the driver had left running, door wide open, in the street. The valet hopped in the pricey wheels, went into reverse and expeditiously parked it within an inch of Emily's old beater.

The Color Launch Party invite said six p.m. to eight p.m. It was a little past six but the showroom was already bursting at the seams with every brand name Los Angeles designer— most of whom would never pass up an open bar at the end of the day. Emily was there for the color presentation and to get a fresh perspective of the color purple. She pushed her way in through the tastefully clad mob and stepped on a few pair of Paul Smith loafers and Gucci boots. No dirty looks in response. It was a cheery crowd.

She snatched the remaining cocktail from the server's tray, barely beating some anonymous hand that almost lay claim to it and made her way over to the refreshments table where some famous design-star faces were playing with the food and laughing it up.

"Excuse me, the paintbrush won't fit in here. Can you tell me how many of these do I need to paint my house?" one marquee designer joked as he held up one of the tiny canapés made in the image of a paint can, complete with logo and paint color name. The dapper group around him chuckled in sync as the famous design expert mimicked opening a can with a penny. They were all wasted and having a fabulous time at the expense of the smart little paint cans.

"Let's do a test color on the wall," a famous dyslexic nightclub designer said, as he smeared a few different little cakes on the wall, then stood back and studied it. "Now, I'd call that a custom blend!"

Just then, yet another noteworthy face came over to join his colleagues. "Oh, I love these, look at all the colors," he said as he picked up some of the paint can snacks and popped several of them in his mouth at once. "Paint never tasted so good."

"Emily Everheart, it's been forever. I recognized those leggy legs of yours in those Prada capris! What a frock star," a drunk design-star said as he fondled the long embroidery lapels on her vintage Galliano. They exchanged hugs and pleasantries and he introduced her to his colleagues.

"I want one of those, but in dusty rose #78. But I think they're all gone," Emily said as she looked at the artful arrangement, stacked by color and size into varying geometrical volumes.

"Oh, that color is way at the bottom. Allow me," the blotto design-star said all gallant-like, as he cautiously removed one tiny dusty rose #78 paint can from the supporting tier and held it up to Emily's face. "It's the same color as your lipstick!"

Emily laughed and he popped the canapé in her open mouth, which made her laugh harder. During this time, others followed the lead and starting raiding the display from the lower level.

"Demolition!" someone yelled.

The display started to sag from the missing pieces and then toppled over completely.

Upon this, everyone cleared the area as if a fire were blazing through. Emily, already feeling the impact of the drink was slow to move out, She was last person remaining at the foot of the disaster, standing and staring at the mess with a look of awe on her face.

"You! You just can't stop harassing me," a voice said from behind her.

Emily turned around. It was her neighbor.

"I appreciate that we are not close, but to wreck my dessert table? You. Bitch. That was the last of what I made. You have ruined my event!"

"It wasn't me."

Candy searched her apron and pulled out a cigarette. She lit it and said, "Well look around. All these people in here look just like you and me. And it wasn't me."

"It was an accident."

"Like hell. Anyone knows that any smear over six inches in length is intentional," Candy said as she pointed to the little pastries smudged on the wall.

"Why are you are so determined to infuriate me?"

"Me infuriate *you*?"

"How could I possibly know you were catering?"

"What does that mean? So if you knew I was the caterer, you would have planned to mutilate my masterpiece? I thought we were square," Candy said, "but apparently I thought wrong," She tried to salvage what she could of the tiny paint cans, picking them up one by one and painstakingly re-sculpting and restacking. Just as Candy realized how hopeless the mess was, Emily, tipsier than thou, burst out a belly laugh.

"Karma. You have earned every ounce of this. You and your veil of ignorance," Emily said.

Candy lunged at Emily and pushed her hard. Emily pushed back harder, sending Candy across the room into the dessert table. They scuffled back and forth awkwardly as if they were in a hurry to get it over with. Candy backed Emily against the wall and used the burning tip of her cigarette as a weapon, holding it close to Emily's face. So close, that Emily feeling the heat raised her hand up to cover her face. Candy jammed the fiery tip into Emily's palm.

Emily screamed and thrust her scorched palm straight into Candy's face with an untamable strength she had no idea she was capable of.

Candy, with a bloody nose, hijacked a porcelain serving platter and hurled it at Emily. She ducked in time and the platter crashed into the wall. The broken shards fired back at her, one striking her face. Emily winced as she unhooked the jagged little splinter and from her cheek. She looked at Candy incredulously.

"You are one very dark and deeply troubled woman," Emily said.

It was no use. Candy wouldn't open her mouth. Her jaw immobile. Her lips impenetrable. Her soul inhospitable. The serum Emily was trying to pour down her throat instead ran down the sides of her face, over her chin and dribbled down her neck. Emily tried in vain to open Candy's mouth to make her drink the truth.

Candy turned her head away, her expression removed from any emotion.

Emily could hear Candy's thought: *You can't poison me.* Candy floated into the air, as if a billowy illusion. Emily reached out in vain to save her neighbor, only to watch helplessly as Candy dissolved into dust, leaving Emily grasping at empty space.

Emily awoke with a jolt and a crashing current of nausea. She flung off the blankets. Quickly and unsteadily, she made her way to the john.

TWELVE

A WEEK LATER, after an early morning, mood enlightening and altering run, Emily stopped by the Seventeenth Street Coffee House to reward herself with some java and one of the most delicious croissants in town.

The runner's high helped in finding her feet in her new steeped-in-gloom-post-Michael-life, and even though there was a vast emptiness in her soul, she was getting use to it. Her new staff would start today, which had given her the previous week to unpack and organize her office— up to a point. The staff would have to help with the rest. She could comfortably work from the loft with a three-person staff, as one of them would most likely be out running errands most of the day.

Thank goodness for Dar, as it was a blessing to be so occupied right now. He was truly an odd bird, and the gallery was far from a dream project, but she would get in, design and produce, and then get out. By that time, the less exotic and more normal clients, like Viv Wyntor, would be approaching her and she could say *adios* to the kooky ones.

She took a seat at an un-bussed table and waited for someone to clean it off and take her order. Along with the dirty plates and half-filled mugs, there was a local throwaway, The *LA Weekly*. When she picked it up, a safety pin fell out and hit the floor. The old Emily would have picked it up. The new Emily noticed and didn't care as she thumbed through the paper, getting glimpses into all these other worlds of nutrition, pollution, holistic health care, medical marijuana and sex therapy. An ad near the front read "Butt Class" and "Rough Leather" next to an article about a big-bra store in Hollywood. Perhaps, she thought, she could get some ideas for the gallery. She stopped at the *Classifinds* and noticed the seemingly endless categories for erotic massage, various acts of foreplay and more butt talk. There were lots of people out there looking for someone to engage in their particular fetish as opposed to a plain old fuck. Forget about searching for a girlfriend, boyfriend, husband, wife or life partner— this wasn't the paper for *those* kinds of ads.

She was amused by what she was reading, but her attention was re-directed when a couple of people at the counter began laughing hysterically at a very animated woman who was obviously regaling them with some great story. The woman, who had her back towards Emily, was holding a large covered basket. She appeared to be doing some kind of schtick: no, it was an imitation. What is this person doing that is so funny, Emily thought, as she watched the cashier and hostess cracking up. She kept watching, thinking she could use a good laugh herself.

There was something about the voice that hit home.

"...and I've been up all night working in metric," the storyteller said in a highly affected, snooty way. "She thinks she's so hot. She's nothing more than a loser. Her Yelp reviews are the worst."

The voice was so familiar in fact that Emily's jaw clenched uncontrollably. She felt her once momentous, neurobiological runner's pleasure vanishing fast. Yelp? Had she heard correctly? Yelp was not her style. She grabbed her phone and self-googled. Sure enough, she was on Yelp. The sad half-one star listing topped the cluttered page and she could make out the words "inauthentic" and "gimmicky" just as she closed out of the page.

"I try to be charitable to her because I feel sorry for her, but it is trying, let me tell you. Oh, and then, I brought her dinner one night, just to be nice, and she didn't eat a fucking thing I made. Another time? You have to hear this— when she first moved in, she smashed my windshield with a baseball bat."

"You should have called the police," The cashier said.

"Yeah, I sure would have. You still can," said the hostess.

There was no doubt that the storyteller could only be one person.

"Well, this is the thing," Candy said sheepishly, as she lowered her voice some, but not so low that Emily couldn't hear. "My windshield had been cracked by some vandals, along with other cars on the street. Since my car hadn't been running for a while, I never did anything about it. I just let it sit in the driveway. Ms. Uptight-Psycho-Ass had just moved in, and the way the hedge hides the car, I guess she couldn't tell it was already cracked. And the kicker is, she gave me three hundred dollars for a new windshield. Can you believe that?"

Both the hostess and the cashier cupped their hands over their noses and mouths, and their eyes went wide in disbelief at Candy's awfulness.

That was it for Emily. Nothing she had done or said so far to Candy justified that vicious back stabbing performance. In fact, she had gone to a lot of trouble to find out how much that windshield cost.

"Here's your order," Candy said as she placed the basket on the counter. "For today, I stuffed them with raspberries and a thyme cream cheese. No one else is doing that anywhere near here," she said as she pointed her finger at the perfect puffy pastries and left without saying good-bye. Emily's eyes followed her out the door until Candy was out of sight, but not out of Emily's mind.

Her thoughts continued to race about the best way to confront Candy; they could have a grown-up conversation, perhaps trace the origin of Candy's misperception of Emily and start fresh— but right then the waitress brought over Emily's pastry and plopped it down in front of her on the still-messy table.

"You must try this, no one else has these," the server said proudly. Emily looked at the plate, where an absolutely perfect example of a croissant sat. She looked back up to the waitress and knew what was coming next.

"Raspberry and thyme cream cheese," the server said with a sweet smile. She then went over to pick up the check from a just vacated table.

"Isn't this lovely," Emily replied flatly to the space where the waitress had been standing.

As she cast her gaze toward the floor, her eyes stopped on something. Making sure no one was looking her way, she dropped her napkin, leaned down discreetly, and grabbed it *and* the safety pin at the same time.

Later that morning Emily was fine-tuning the office space and laying out the workstations. The former living room would now accommodate Darren, Beth and Kimiko.

She was moving Kimiko's desk closer to the window to take advantage of natural daylight, when there was a sudden commotion upstairs. She could hear Candy on the phone, as both their windows were open. Candy was speaking quite loudly and from what Emily could overhear, she sounded quite defensive. Emily went over to the window, right under where Candy was standing, to better hear exactly what was going on.

"How long have we been doing business together? Have we ever had a problem before? I don't believe a word of this. What do you mean you saw it with your own eyes? Impossible!" Candy's always-cheerful voice was raised and angry. Then Emily heard Candy saying, "No, you can't cut me off over this. You are wrong! I'll prove it to you. I will get to the bottom of this."

Candy sounded panicked now. Serves her right, Emily thought as she continued to eavesdrop.

"No, please don't do that, do not call the health department."

Emily almost lost it at that! In fact she had to cover her mouth to keep from bursting out into laughter. She held her breath to hear the rest of the conversation.

"At least allow me to defend myself. My reputation is on the line. You have to tell me who did this. Somebody put a safety pin in my croissant," Candy said to the person at the other end of the phone, as she stomped on the floor, shaking the light fixture over Emily's head.

Emily quietly backed away from the window and started unpacking the office supplies.

"Now *that's* a kicker," she said out loud.

THIRTEEN

CANDY THREW THE PHONE across the kitchen. It landed on its end, half submerged in a giant stainless steel bowl filled with batter. She paced back and forth while her head spun with all kinds of solutions to remedy the disaster. The Eighteenth Street Coffee House had cut her off, just like that. The so-called "victim" had made a big scene. She said she was stabbed in the mouth with a filthy, germ-laden safety pin hidden in her raspberry and thyme cream cheese croissant and was now suffering mental anguish. The bakery was only one of her many accounts, but the Westside pastry world was small and highly competitive. It was crawling with fresh-faced cake designers as well as the established houses. Candy knew as of this moment the odds were great that her slot was about to be re-filled and her reputation was on the road to being tarred. If she didn't act very soon, in addition to being rebuffed and replaced, she would be completely forgotten.

She poured herself a beer and decided she would be proactive starting now. First, she would calm down. Then she would go back to The Eighteenth Street Coffee House in the morning and ask for another chance. And, she would give them a week's worth of pastries *gratis*.

Candy continued preparing the batch of her new fruity beauty apricot cake. The pans were papered and greased and she just had to add the final bit of ginger root, when she had been interrupted by the unsettling phone call. Trying hard to re-focus, she concentrated on the recipe. While the union of apricot and ginger was inspired, finding the perfect proportions of these two star ingredients was tricky.

With her tasting pinkie, she popped a smidgen of the mixture in to her mouth, then rapidly flicked her tongue around the flavor palette. Could use a boozy riff, she mused, and then augmented the batter with shot of apple brandy. Edible perfection indeed— a winner. She sloppily scribbled this annotation in the margin of the recipe book, then added "try pumping like-flavored jam into wall cake" and dated it.

Downstairs, Toshi, a friend of Kimiko Arada, who would be upgrading the computer network and all related tech-orating systems for an hourly fee, had arrived a tad early and waited outside for her. She was right on time and they went inside together. Toshi started on his computer task, while Kimiko helped Emily unpack boxes of support-staff stuff and resource material, much of which was obsolete now that everyone was sourcing on-line. Emily had kept physical catalogs and control samples around because she wasn't the best internet surfer, not having grown up with it. She still relied on tools she could pick up and touch and relish in the ritual of an unhurried study. Still, she hoped her new young staff would help bring her e-office protocol up to date. Kimiko had been shocked that someone still kept catalogs, but embraced it as a retro idea.

Darren was next to arrive and jumped right in with the unpacking. The last to show up was Beth Konisberg, who was disgusted when she saw the catalogs. Was she supposed to work with those old soiled, dog-eared things? She picked up a catalog and then dropped it, holding her hands in the air as if the binder was smeared with shit. She made a face and found her way to the bathroom to wash the offending grime off her hands.

Upon Beth's return, Emily showed the staff around the place, briefing them about the office routines. Kimiko would handle the resources, front office, e-design and CAD. Beth would cover design, drawing, color and materials as well as work e-design. Darren would handle the fieldwork and assist Emily across the board. Each staff member's time would be billed back to the project at rates commensurate to the task.

The upstairs distraction of baking equipment banging around was irritatingly audible. Kimiko was focused on Emily's instruction and was able to transcend the clatter. Not so for Beth. "What's going on up there?" she blurted, interrupting Emily.

"You'll have to ignore it. It's noisy up there. That's just the way it is." Emily added, "Hopefully it won't go on too much longer."

Beth huffed. Everyone looked at her.

There was a knock at the door. Kimiko answered it and returned with a Fed-X containing Dar Aroubian's signed Letter of Agreement and the $70,000 design fee retainer.

Emily was relieved. Until you had the signed contract and the retainer, you were always taking a risk by proceeding. Now Project Dar was officially official. "Okay, staff," Emily announced, "Let's put this thing on The Board and pull the trigger. Darren, verify the field measurements and conditions at the site first thing tomorrow morning."

For no apparent reason, Beth began bossing Kimiko around. Not wanting to disrupt harmony, Kimiko ignored her and kept on with her organizing the design library. Beth's audacity caught Emily's attention.

"To repeat, you all report to me; there is no hierarchy here other than that. No bullying, no alpha behavior, no gossiping, no backstabbing. We are a team that works closely together and supports one another. Anyone who doesn't carry his or her weight won't last around here. I have zero tolerance for bullshit, bluffing, lies and other unbalanced behavior. If you are under the illusion that I am even-tempered, think again. When I get to the point of exploding, I can assure you that none of you will want to witness that. Am I clear?"

Just then, another loud, sharp, crashing sound came from upstairs, undermining Emily's lecture. "Damn her, I should kill her. I sure could use the extra space," Emily said under her breath.

Kimiko kept her nose in her task at hand, and Beth opened her mouth as if to challenge Emily, but thought better of it and went back to working alongside Kimiko, unpacking the product catalogs and various product samples. They would make sure all the material was current and recycle the obsolete information and duplicates. Tedious, it was, and that was an understatement. It was something Emily should have done before she moved to the new space, but she had been in such a funk over Michael that she was unable to be anywhere near organized. Her heart felt heavy as she looked at the pile of discards. Parting with these outdated things was saying good-bye to her old life and, in particular, to Michael. She knew she would always love him, even when he would be nothing more than a distant memory. Why she kept him alive in her heart, which gave her little comfort, she just couldn't figure out. She knew she had no choice but to move on and—

"These look personal. Where should they go?" Beth asked, interrupting Emily's thoughts. Beth was holding up some faded photos of Emily and Michael.

Emily stared at them and then said, "The trash bin. Take them out with all the other garbage."

Emily then called the group together for a status meeting to familiarize them with all the current projects.

"As you know, I am offering a new e-design service. We'll try it out for a while and see how it goes. Many consumers prefer working this way nowadays. I am not sure if those consumers are our demographic, but let's find out," Emily said. "Toshi will design a portion of the website to accommodate the interest. Once we qualify the leads, I'll turn the projects over to Kimiko and Beth."

"What about the fee structure?" Beth asked.

"I am reviewing some standards that are out there right now," Emily said.

"How much time should we spend on e-projects?" Kimiko asked.

"Depends on the scope. I'd say, off-hand, work as efficiently as possible and call it a day. The work will have to be good enough, not the best, because there is no way we can judge the complexities of a space on-line. Standards are relaxing. People are finding less detail and lower quality acceptable these days. It's a new frontier for us, so we will all have to re-think how we work and adapt, Emily said. "I'll also need to have disclaimers left, right and center on the agreements. Kimiko, please make a note to remind me of that."

"Are we giving up the traditional working structure?" Beth asked, with a look of shock.

"No. There is still a lot of work out there. I know my market and I go after it. But soon, even that niche will die off," Emily, pragmatic.

"Okay, next on the list is a custom wine cellar for a new client, Ms. Wyntor. And some rugs just after that. So these are two, small, high quality tasks for right now. I have a feeling there could be more once she becomes comfortable with us." Emily covered the specifics about the project and assigned Kimiko to refine Emily's free-hand sketches on CAD. Then Emily went on in detail about the Gallery and what was needed to be done next. She asked Darren to catalogue the artwork that Dar would be displaying at the Gallery. Everyone's eyes lit up when Emily showed them the same presentation with which she had wowed Dar. The meeting ended with a standing ovation topped off with fist-bumps all around.

At the end of business, Emily watched out of the corner of her eye as Kimiko and Beth grabbed the trash bags and hauled them out back to the bin. *I will not, I will not,* Emily chanted silently to herself. *I will not go out there. I will not go out there to retrieve the photos.* Kimiko and Beth crossed paths with Candy at the trash bins.

"Hey, if you gals see a phone out here, it belongs to me. It must have gotten mixed up in the trash. I can't find it anywhere," Candy said, as she dumped over the bulky, plastic contraptions and picked over the rotting refuse. "Just leave your trash bags there and I'll put them in the bin when I'm done looking."

"Fine with me," Beth said slightly exasperated, to anyone who could hear. She was relieved she wouldn't have to touch a grimy old trashcan. "I wasn't told that hauling trash was in my job description." She dropped the large bag right where she was standing and turned around to go back to the office to wash her hands. Again. Kimiko placed her bags down gently next to the bins, then turned and started to walk away.

"Do you live around here?" Candy asked. "I don't recognize you."

Kimiko shook her head and pointed at Emily's place. "We work there."

Candy looked surprised. "Well she could have told me about that. Now she'll have all these characters coming and going throughout the day. There goes any peace and quiet I had."

"Why don't you call your phone?" Kimiko suggested to Candy, who looked at her like she was speaking Martianese. "To hear it ring," Kimiko added slowly and loudly, then headed back toward the office without uttering another word.

"Good idea," Candy said with her back to Kimiko as she now waded through all the garbage she had rifled and strewn about. Her eyes landed on Emily's trash bags. What the hell, she thought....

As she picked up the bag that Beth had dropped, the bottom seam split and everything spilled out. Candy bent over wanting to take a good look at what Emily was throwing out. Maybe there would be something good that she could use. Disappointed that it was only outdated catalogs and papers, she continued to dig until she came across some photographs of Emily and some guy, obviously the Ex. Candy could see that the photographs were from much happier times and that the Ex was quite good looking. He must be why Emily is always in such a mood, she thought. On closer inspection, the frames were certainly worth keeping. They would make gorgeous cake and cookie trays for her dessert book photography. She then remembered why she was in the trash pile in the first place.

"Hey, call my phone. I'll listen for it," Candy called out to Kimiko, as if it were her own idea. She looked back to see a wisp of dark hair and a sleeve of a jean jacket duck inside the rear office door as it closed. Candy followed her. Once inside at Emily's, she saw that no one was in the rear of the loft, so she made her way to the front. Candy looked around, surprised at how different it was starting to look. She went over to Kimiko's desk and spotted a check for $70K made out to EEID. She noted the name on the check.

Something red caught her eye at the adjacent desk. It was a simply shaped container with an exquisite form. The inspiration struck her at first glimpse— a perfect form for her green tea mousse. This was just the type of object she needed. She made a beeline to Beth's station, snatched it and went back to Kimiko's desk.

Just then Kimiko returned and saw Candy at her desk, holding Beth's red container. Before Kimiko could say anything, Candy said, "I'm going to borrow this."

"It's not mine," Kimiko said.

Then Candy picked up Emily's cell phone, which was also on Kimiko's desk and punched in her number.

"Hey! That's mine and it's sentimental." Beth said still drying her hands from the germ eradicating washing. "What are you doing with it?"

"I'll give it back. Call me in thirty seconds," Candy said as she zipped out the back door. She made a detour to fetch Emily's discarded frames and photos, then clunked up the staircase back home.

Toshi came out from under Kimiko's desk, where he had been fiddling with a connection the whole time. He'd been updating Emily's cell phone programming. As it was now already a few minutes after quitting time, and eager to leave, Kimiko hit the send button which would give that crazy lady sixty seconds to find her phone. She had already said good-bye to Emily and she and Toshi would soon be on their way to meet some friends for Happy Hour on Sawtelle Boulevard.

Candy traced the muffled ring to a loaf pan filled with the chocolate-ginger-apricot mixture that apparently never made it into the oven. She managed to fish the phone out of the batter and rinse it off, without having the courtesy to say hello and thank you to Kimiko. The remaining concoction appeared fine, so she would later pop it in the oven with the rest of the loaf pans.

Candy was jazzed about the red box. She would have to deconstruct it, to make a pattern from the parts and then reassemble it and return it to that girl. On second thought, the shape was so precise that she knew she'd have to sacrifice the box entirely to get it perfect. She was also elated about finding the frames. They were just right. That Emily sure had lots of inspiring objects scattered about her place.

Emily, alone now, was finishing up for the day. They were off to an acceptable start and very soon they would be fine-tuned as a team. The only hiccup was that Beth had rubbed her the wrong way. She wasn't the same person Emily had interviewed twice. Emily was counting on the fact that Beth was just having an off day.

FOURTEEN

CANDY COULD SMELL a health department official at five hundred yards. Panicked, she was working quickly to get her kitchen in order— well, as ordered as possible in the hope that she wouldn't be shut down for operating a bootlegged bakery. She would give her it all before going down the tubes. She would try to sweet-talk the official with one of her aphrodisiac layer cakes and some dessert wine, and maybe have *ESPN* or porno running on the television. She could dress up and put on make up, too. Eyeliner in abundance got them every time (like that *Malcolm* episode when Lois gets a makeover). The only problem was, she had no idea when he (or she) would show up so she would have to be ready to put the moves on at a moment's notice.

Candy started with the freezer. She dated everything with yesterday's date and made sure everything was wrapped tight and clean. Finishing her current project, the Wall Cake, would have to wait. The sections were ready to be assembled, frosted and decorated for the Minuteman Ball tomorrow— a referral from the NRA Right to Carry Banquet, where the Marzipan Uzi centerpiece had been a huge smash. She would have to get to that first thing in the morning. First things first: save her kitchen no matter what.

She checked availability on all the necessary props— cake, beer and porno on demand. That, combined with a little luck, was the recipe for an amenable outcome.

While she was cleaning, organizing and adjusting shelf dates and temperatures her mind wandered to the fat check she saw at

Emily's. This tweaked her the more she thought about it. Candy was capable of pulling in seventy grand, but only if she slogged endless hours— twice as intense as most other pastry creators. This irked her deep down because she knew she toiled unquestionably harder than that Emily. Why, she hadn't seen Emily do anything but bitch and whine since she had moved in. And adding insult to injury, "retainer" was written in the line on the front of the check. That meant there was more money to come! That client must be loaded, *and* a spender. Candy decided she would track him down to see if he were interested in a baked goods daily delivery to his company. His name had slipped from her mind for the moment, but it would come back to her. She had all night to clean up— it was past the end of business hours for the city, so no doubt an inspector would be here early tomorrow.

Later that evening, Emily met Linda Sterling at Harvelle's. When they got there, they found out it was open microphone night.

"I don't know about this. What do you think?" Emily said.

"You never know around here. *Bob Dylan* could show up," Linda said. "Or *Neil Young*."

"I follow this scene a lot. My problem is, I always seem to be here for the fake version, or the untalented sibling with the famous last name," Emily said.

"Well, sometimes it's not so bad. I have a feeling tonight we'll hear some talent. I just sense it."

A young couple left the bar and Linda made a beeline for the vacated seats. It was quite dark inside, and several middle aged to really old age dudes and dudettes were hanging out, having a few drinks. The music didn't start for another half hour, but the energy was upbeat.

The bartender came their way. "That guy back there wants to buy your drinks." He pointed to the opposite end of the room.

"We're fine, really," Emily said.

"Speak for yourself," Linda said. "A guy like that just wants someone to talk to, not to pick up. These old guys are just happy to see a female or two that won't yell at them."

"OK, two Cosmos please," Emily said. Turning to Linda she said, "And why won't we yell at them?"

"Because we aren't their wives or girlfriends. Because we don't give a flying fuck."

"I never yelled at Michael," Emily said.

"In your case, you should have, that was one of your problems. You were too nice to Michael. And you still are too nice for your own good," Linda said. "You have to be more of a bitch. But not with me."

Just then Mr. Borderline-Homeless-looking-drink-buying-man came towards them to strike up a conversation— or rather to cut to the chase and ask them (yes, both of them) out. Emily looked at Linda, who twisted a *who knew?* expression on her face.

"How about a Kings game?"

"No way. I got hit with the puck in the head at the last hockey game I went to," Linda said.

"Okay, how about a Dodger game?"

"Nope. The last baseball game I went to the people in the seats above me spilled beer and nachos on me."

"Well, then how about a football game....somewhere?" Pig-man asked.

"Uh uh. I got trampled by an angry mob at Super Bowl XXIII."

He turned to Emily. Before he could say anything she blurted, "Three strikes, you are out." He digested the comment, nodded, turned and walked away.

"Well, I guess you spoke a language he understood," Linda said as she held up her glass to Emily's. "But you were still way too nice about it."

The open mic talent that evening was anemic and uneventful. The final straw was an off-key, 21-year old singing an acoustic version of *Highway To Hell*. "She's got to be somebody's little dar-lin'," Linda said. "There is no way anyone would have her play when there are so many super talented musicians around. And her guitar was way too real-deal hip. It was a vintage *Martin*. You just know it's Dad's guitar. Or Mom's."

As they walked out of Harvelle's, *John Densmore* walked in. There was no mistaking him for anyone else. The girls stopped in their tracks as it registered and did double takes. But by then the door had closed.

They headed over to Hal's in Venice for a late dinner.

They took Fourth Street over the freeway, turned right on Pico to Main Street, then left on Main. Linda ran a red to make the left on Abbot Kinney and parked a block away from Hal's. They jay-walked across Abbott Kinney and stopped to look in the window of a trendy vintage furniture shop where everything was painted a peeling white or rust eaten at the edges, and, all of it over-priced.

Hal's was packed, but they managed to get a booth as a group had just finished dining and everyone else wanted to stay in the front bar. Walking to their booth, they checked out the action in the bar. Linda waved to some people she knew.

"Who's that?" Emily asked as they sat down.

"My agent and her assistant, Brett. I don't know the two guys talking to them. They look like twins."

Emily glanced over at them, and then went back to the menu. "They sure do look alike. Why don't you go and say hello to your agent and get a closer look?"

"It can wait," Linda said, "She's going to say, 'You should be writing. What are you doing out and about?' and I don't want to hear that right now. Besides, she looks quite involved in their con-versation. She could use a tumble with one of those guys, or both. Do twins count as one or two?"

"Depends if it's simultaneous or consecutive," Emily responds straight faced.

"Speaking from experience?"

"There are just some things you take to the grave with you."

The waiter came over. "Those two guys in the lounge would like to buy you two a drink," he said with a nod toward the lounge end of the bar, opposite from where Linda's agent and the twins were chatting.

"Must be our night. And we're not even blonde," Linda said as she flipped her fingers through her hair.

Emily and Linda looked at each other for a beat, shrugged and placed their order for round two of Cosmos, without looking over at the lounge to acknowledge their benefactors.

"This must be what's called a grey pick-up. They probably think we are an easy mark because we're older and oh so desperate," Emily said.

"Or lesbians."

"Or beyond getting pregnant— worry free."

"We're more relaxed than youngsters because we don't have the same priorities. We don't have to worry about *One*— If our parents will approve of him, *Two*— Will he be a good father/husband/provider, *Three*— If we are the same religion, *Four*— If we have anything in common, *Five*— What our kids would look like, what I mean is, is he from a bunch of Frankenstein look-alikes. Really, would you want your potential daughter to look like Frankenstein? *Six*— Do we want to grow old with him and change his diapers. At our age, all we want is a nice time with a nice guy. We don't want them to stick around and be all needy-ass and grumpy. Hell, sometimes I think I ain't gonna touch another one for years."

The drinks arrived and they turned to courtesy toast in the direction of the drink buyers, who had, by this time, been making their way over to the booth and were now in earshot of Linda's explanation as to why older women are such happening things. The forty-ish, tad-conservative, mid-range handsome, corporately groomed duo, wore facial expressions of shock and disgust.

"But women still want a man who can be a good partner," the taller one, seriously and clearly offended, said directly to Linda. "I wouldn't have believed this drivel if I hadn't heard it myself."

"It seems it would take more than we could offer to make them happy," the other tall one said, equally offended.

"They're way too bitter for us," the first tall man said to his friend, giving the girls a disdainful once over. "And way too old, now that I see them up close."

At a loss to understand Emily and Linda's attitudes, one of them snatched the Cosmos away, spilling some on Linda's hair. Then they turned and walked over to another table of dewy, bubbly, young women drinking *champagne-in-a-can* who invited them to sit down. The young women really fussed over the two men with a carefree and anything-goes type of attitude and responded with lilted laughter to whatever the men had to say.

"Those guys are one big snooze," Linda said to Emily as she dried off her hair with her napkin.

Emily glared at Linda. "It's a good thing I'm not into meeting anyone right now otherwise I would throttle you."

"Oh, they're way too serious for us, anyhow," Linda said.

"Maybe so, but we were just in the presence of not only potential stud material, but potential long term relationship, maybe even marriage, material. That's a very rare combination that doesn't often come along around here. I know it when I see it. And, there are two of them. Make that, *were* two of them," Emily said as their food arrived.

"I know that. Don't forget I am capable of identifying such traits in men. I had a good one— the best, for 20 years and those are big shoes to fill. I haven't met anyone who comes close to filling them— not even those two semi-perfect looking schmos. You know as well as I what men put women through, so we have to make sure whoever it is who puts us through all that shit, that they are worth it. If I am lucky enough to have another chance at true love I will take it. I don't want to drive a good man away anymore than you do.

"But, any guy worth his salt would have laughed it up with us after hearing what I said. Those two humorless blobs couldn't put three words together to express themselves. The best they did was get appalled at us. You and I both need someone wittier and faster on their feet than—"

"You didn't come over. We must talk," Judy Cleveland scolded Linda, leaving Emily indistinguishable as a crumb. "Any updates for me on your fabulous book? I can't tell you how excited we are about it. You are a literary star. You are the next—"

"Judy Cleveland, this is my best friend, Emily Everheart," Linda said.

"You know Sony is interested in the film rights," Judy went on, not missing a beat, and not even a glance toward Emily. "And they're not the only ones. I smell a bidding war. I hear Meagan Fox wants to do it right after Transformers 6. That's huge. Do you have any idea how huge that is?"

"Judy, all that is just great. I'm so happy you're on the ball and have only my best interests in mind, but Emily and I have a bet that the guys you and Brett were chatting up at the bar are twins," Linda asked, wanting to change the subject. She was tired of hearing Judy go on about how late the book is and how fabulous everything is and all the C and D level talent she was trying to attach to the sale.

Judy twitched. She had to think for a moment of something other than her lit business. She turned to Brett Hyatt, who had active cell phone conversations at each of his ears, with a questioning look on her face. "The guys at the bar?"

The Harvard double MBA nodded and mouthed the word *twins*.

"Oh, *those* twins. Brett arranged the meeting with them through the maitre'd at *Nobu* as a favor. You know one must keep a maitre'd happy. I wasn't at all interested in them or their schlock treatment about time traveling, twin, bodybuilding, midget Mossad agents. They gave me their card. I can't believe Brett wasted my time like that," Judy said, tossing the card on the tabletop.

Then she, Brett, and his two cell phone conversations turned abruptly and left. Brett Hyatt transferred both cell phones to the same ear to free up his other hand to get the door for Judy Cleveland.

"Now do you get it why I didn't want to talk to her," Linda said, as they were getting ready to leave.

"Do you think she saw me at all?" Emily asked.

"Well, it's not that she didn't see you. It's that she saw you, but didn't need to talk to you because you can't do anything for her in her business, so therefore, you don't exist to her. So yeah, you are right, she didn't see you. I wouldn't worry about it."

"Oh, I'm not," Emily said, as they left. Just as they got to the front door, the waiter came after them and was waving something they left on the table. Emily, thinking it was her credit card, reached out to take it. Not recognizing it, she looked closer and saw it was the twins' business card. Absentmindedly, she shoved it in her pocket.

FIFTEEN

THE NEXT MORNING Emily met Darren at the job site to go over the sprawling canvas of naked space. She had instructed Beth Konisberg to be there to help out and also to document the meeting details. Upon entering, Emily was pleased with Dar's choice of building. She could see the great potential. It was pure and classic— spacious with soaring ceilings and great light quality. A vintage parquetry wood floor and plaster frieze relief reminded her of its past splendors. A recent retrofit had upgraded all the building systems. Additionally, having a design project with a prominent Beverly Hills address, in a historic, adaptive re-use space, was a good thing for her. Wealthy people often assumed (not always correctly) that Beverly Hills reflected the city's best design projects. Besides, having to go into Beverly Hills was just plain nice, it was a beautiful city with much to offer.

As Beth was late, Darren and Emily started the meeting. They didn't want to fall behind in the day's schedule. They had been analyzing the natural light and how to take advantage of it in the gallery when Beth strolled in, holding a Starbucks. "Traffic was terrible," she said quite seriously, looking straight at Emily as if it were Emily's fault traffic was bad.

Emily didn't waste any time getting Beth started. "We don't have any recent as-builts to work from. Darren's measuring out the electrical and phone locations right now. You can start measuring the overall length and width of each area. I have a conference call I have to jump on in five minutes. You *do* have your tape measure?"

"Right here," Beth said, as she leisurely placed her *venti* soy latte on the aged parquetry and went into her purse. She pulled out a tiny metal disc that housed the smallest tape measure that Emily and Darren had ever seen in their professional lives. The span was a mere sixty inches. Darren got a concerned look on his face but didn't say anything.

"You can't possibly use that," Emily said. "Don't you have an appropriate tape measure?" Anyone in the business always carried or kept near by, *very* near by, a Stanley twenty-five footer or the slightly less accurate laser measure.

"I wouldn't be able to close my purse if I had a bigger one," Beth said quite seriously. Darren was about to get outraged, but kept his cool.

"Then get a bigger purse," Emily said, as she tossed her tape to Beth. "Don't ever show up at a job site with that little thing again. You'll waste so much time, and time is money. We won't have this conversation again."

The tape had old drywall mud caked on it that flaked off when Beth caught it. And the edge of the tape, jagged in places, would require careful handling so she wouldn't cut herself or, more importantly, snag her clothes on it. She gingerly held it between her thumb and forefinger and went about measuring. Beth didn't understand why Emily got so upset over a tape measure. She would use this honker of a device, so be it, so not to push her boss over the edge. She liked this firm, and the project, and wanted to stay for a while. She would certainly have to wash her hands after using the dirty old thing.

Emily walked to a quiet corner of the space. The conference call wasn't for a few minutes yet so she called Kimiko at the office to check in.

"Emily Everheart Design," Kimiko answered with a heavy accented but, otherwise, good English.

"It's Emily, Kimiko," Emily said, "Any messages?"

"Well...yes. The woman said we have too many computers and they are interfering with her signal making her signal very slow. She came here and unplugged some things. She's very mad," Kimiko said.

"What woman?" Emily didn't know whom Kimiko could have been speaking about.

"The woman upstairs."

There was a pause in the conversation. Emily took a deep breath and tried to compose her thoughts before she spoke. For Emily to be outraged would have been an understatement. Gone for an hour and a half and Candy had managed to find her way into intruding upon Kimiko and Toshi, disrupting business.

"Our system has nothing to do with her place," Emily said, even though she knew she should be having this conversation with Candy and not Kimiko.

"So Toshi went up to look at her system. Then there were loud noises and yelling," Kimiko said, sounding troubled, but not wanting to let on that she was. She wanted to be able to handle the office and the foot traffic that would come and go.

"What happened?"

"I don't know. He's still up there, and there is still much noise," Kimiko said.

Emily could feel her blood pressure rising and was about to tell Kimiko to go get Toshi when her call waiting beeped. The caller ID said it was Dar, which meant the conference call with him and the contractor, Frank Thorney, was beginning. Completely frazzled, she hung up on Kimiko, took the incoming call and tried to re-focus. It wasn't easy, especially since the call opened with the contractor blindsiding her— bad-mouthing and blaming Emily for running rogue and designing a space that will be way too costly to build out, that will result in delays and huge cost overruns, and how he was going to have to dumb down her design concept in order to build at the cost he had quoted Dar previously, and even then he didn't think the gallery would function efficiently. Furthermore, Dar should always have fresh flowers in the lobby and there was no place in the lobby that allowed for fresh flowers, and that even he, a contractor, knows about fresh flowers, but why doesn't Emily, the irresponsible interior designer, know that—

"No, stop right there," Emily interrupted, with the fumes from her conversation with Kimiko fueling her agitation, "I'm sorry you are not up to the task, Frank, but Dar has approved this upgrade to his asset. This is a cutting edge project that has to stand on its own and make a statement. Dar knows this is not only a financial commitment but also a design commitment that requires a skilled builder, who can execute this custom work correctly and build out this design within the budget.

"Dar, I can refer you to several generals, who do great quality work, who won't low bid just to get the job and who are not only interested in lining their own pockets." Emily's call-waiting beeped. It beeped again. She hit the ignore button and sent it into voicemail as she saw from the caller ID it was Kimiko, and had no choice but to let her leave a message. That situation would have to wait.

"Hey lady, lighten up. I was just fooling around. You don't have to be so serious," Frank said with a forced laugh. "If I'd have known you'd take it the wrong way I wouldn't have started the meeting off with a joke. Too bad, so sad, your loss. Geeez. Go have a beer."

"Oh, please. Grow up," Emily said, knowing now that Frank was a liar *and* a schmuck *and* trying to back-peddle out of the situation by blaming it on her. He wasn't the first troublemaker, nor would he be the last, to act that way— to try to be the hero to the client at the designer's expense.

"Hey, that's uncalled for. What have I ever done to you? You have zero sense of humor, lady," Frank said.

"Dar," Emily said, ignoring Frank, "Are you still on the line?"

"Here I am," he said. He was multi tasking over some documents, but now focused back on the conference call. "Let's drop the love-fest and get on with the meeting. Nobody is going anywhere. You'll work together because I want it that way. A little antagonism can be healthy. I just don't want to hear about it," Dar said from his cell phone at 36,000 feet.

"Between the two of you, you'll figure it out. I expect a big return on my investment and I know you won't let me down," Dar said, then ended the conference call with them, but immediately called Emily afterwards.

"Just work with him on this project. He's my half-brother's step-kid and no one knows what to do with him. We pass him back and forth— it's a family obligation. It'll be fine, he's just a dumb asshole, nothing more or less. I do think he can build, but he'll need direction," Dar said.

"You *think* he can build?" The call-waiting beeped. Again it was the office and again Emily sent the call into voicemail, not giving it a second thought.

"This is his first real project. I'm told he was always digging holes in people's yards," Dar said, "And he has a bizarre fascination for sawing wood, especially oak."

"He's obviously incapable of handling the building inspectors—"

"Don't worry about that. My family has been in this neighborhood for a long time," Dar said. Emily got what he meant, so she was able to at least get past the *City* concern.

"I'll collaborate, but tutoring and babysitting an ADHD, emotionally stunted oaf of a general contractor isn't what I do," Emily said.

"You'll do a great job! Get more people if you have to. Just keep track of the extra time and I'll let Andrea know we had this conversation. Now, I have a change of plans on Phase Two Asset. I'm not going to buy the coastal property in Costa Rica. They kidnap people like me down there, so I have a better plan. I've found this great parcel in Arizona."

"What about the spread in Texas you were thinking about?" Emily asked.

"My cell phone wouldn't work there so I backed out of that deal. I didn't want to get involved in buying a tower just for me.

Anyway, I am on my way to see the Arizona parcel right now. I'll tell you all about it when the deal is closed. Now, it's time for my lunch," Dar said from above the clouds as he poured a package of Emergen-C into a strawberry daiquiri.

Toshi was trembling as he sent the text message to Kimiko. He was not leaving the shower stall because the lady had told him she would kill him if he tried to get out. He was not sure what this was all about, so he decided it might be better to wait it out. For what or whom, he didn't quite know. She wasn't the first oddball he had run into. Americans could be so bizarre.

He had come upstairs to try to help the lady with her computer problem because he thought it was something simple like an unplugged modem or a case of needing to reboot. He knew that the system he had hooked up downstairs had nothing to do with the woman's problem upstairs. He was just trying to help an older lady, to be nice, nothing more. He hoped Emily wouldn't find out about this. He didn't want to lose a new client, one that could refer him to many others. After all, she was paying him to work for her, not to work upstairs. He would just come in, fix it quickly, and leave. Easy as anything, he had thought.

But these computer terminals were a mess and unsafely plugged in to code-violating outlets— not to mention her entire system caused him concern. She had an old, out-of-date Wang computer, with a pile of similar models she had purchased on-line for spare parts. That way, she would never have to learn to use another kind of computer. Upon seeing all this, Toshi, heavily experienced in the variety of tech-dinosaurs, immediately knew the user profile: Deep Rooted Hard Drive Psychosis. Cheapness had nothing to do with it since one could buy even a *Mac* on EBay for fifty bucks. That meant to him to get out of there as fast as he could. It was amazing what insight into someone's head you could diagnose just by their computer hardware.

But just after Toshi had arrived, someone had knocked at the lady's door, which caused her to get all nervous and irritated.

That's when she pushed Toshi into the bathroom, shoved him into the shower and threatened to kill him, as she backed away with a crazed expression on her face. He couldn't see anything but heard lots of banging and thumping and a heated conversation about what he couldn't quite tell, which at times got louder and then would die back.

Kimiko texted back that Emily had just called and he better get back downstairs right now. Toshi could have sworn he heard a man's voice, but it was hard to tell. He was afraid to move, and his mind ran to paranoid thinking that maybe the person with the booming voice would beat him up, or kill him. He didn't know what to think. He texted back to Kimiko that he would be down in a few minutes, but if he didn't get there soon, to come up and get him. He warned her that it might not be safe, so she should be very careful and bring something she could use as a weapon.

Kimiko's eyes widened as she got to the end of Toshi's text. Alarmed, she called Emily right away, but it went into voice mail, with the outgoing message saying Emily was on the other line. A few minutes later she tried again and got the same message. She decided to text Emily. Having never discussed texting with her new boss, she wasn't sure the office etiquette included text messaging. She thought about it for a few moments and decided to go for it. After all, Toshi might be in real danger.

Emily's head was still swirling from the conference call. Dar had dropped the good news on her that there was another big project in the near future. She was jazzed about it, so the thought of the idiot half-step nephew GC took a back seat to that. What a roller coaster of a morning, she thought. Just then her phone made an unfamiliar sound. She looked at the screen and it said something about a message waiting for her. It was a new phone and Emily hadn't mastered all of its capabilities.

"Beth, can you show me how to access a text message?" as Emily held out her phone. Beth stopped in her tracks and just stared at it.

"I don't touch other people's phones," Beth said with a look that clearly read *Germ Phobic*. Wasn't using this gross tape measure torture enough? What did Emily expect of her?

Just then Darren came up from behind and plucked the phone from Emily's hand. "Here you go. It's easy, you just touch the envelope icon like so and here's the message, *'Toshi's in danger upstairs call me & come back, help, Kimiko,'* and it ends with a cute little distressed emoji.

"That can't be right. Let's read it again. No, it *is* right," Darren said as he looked at Emily.

Emily grabbed her phone and hit the speed dial to the office. After four rings, it went into voicemail. She didn't leave a message. Her hands were trembling so she had Darren text back to Kimiko saying Emily was enroute to the office and to wait for her before doing anything else.

"Don't worry about us, we'll finish up here just fine and catch up with you later," Darren said to Emily, who stumbled over Beth's coffee, spilling it all over the vintage inlaid floor, as she headed out of the building.

Beth looked at Darren and said, "Would you look at that! I wasn't finished my latte! I gather Kimiko has caused some trouble. Can you believe Emily had to go back there? What a waste of her time," Beth said as she looked around the building. "And this space isn't exactly the *d'Orsay*."

"*Le* d'Orsay has Haystacks and Wheatfields. We have boobs and butts. What do you expect? Now clean up that mess and let's get back to the survey," Darren said, incensed. He handed her a tiny digital camera. "Take some pictures. One in each direction of each space, and I'll need the ceilings as well."

"Who made you boss?" Beth muttered under her breath as she grudgingly mopped up the spill with her foot and a cache of napkins that she had stockpiled from Starbucks. Her boss should have been more careful, she thought.

SIXTEEN

EMILY MADE IT ACROSS TOWN in only twenty minutes, which wasn't a common event these days, since the previous decade of over-building and neglected traffic problems had left the city broken. As she got out of her car and headed toward the loft, she scrutinized the exterior of the building. From her point of view, nothing appeared out of order. In fact, it seemed rather tranquil.

Emily's front door was open. Upon entering she saw Kimiko and a well-to-do looking woman of her own age in a conversation.

"Emily, this is Ms. Goodman," Kimiko said, a bit flustered, but managing to maintain her composure. "She wants to meet with you to discuss her Beverly Hills Park home. Ms. Goodman, please meet Emily Everheart."

Beverly Park was what Kimiko had meant to say. Said area consisted of very large, new homes. Said area was enough to make any designer stop in his or her brand-name tracks. This day was certainly made up of curve balls. Despite the fact that Emily was on a mission to get Toshi back from Candy, she was able to be professional— moving from panic mode into business mode. She had learned long ago to be able to switch gears at the drop of a hat. She softened her facial expression and reached out her hand to formally greet Ms. Goodman.

"It's a pleasure to meet you. Thank you for coming by," Emily said, shaking her hand, trying to concentrate on Ms. Goodman while wondering about Toshi's well being. "Would you excuse me for just a moment? I have to run upstairs for something. Kimiko, will you make Ms. Goodman some tea, please?"

"Well, I haven't much time," Ms. Goodman said. "I know I stopped by unannounced, but I happened to be in the neighborhood. I loved the house you did in Architectural Digest last year. I meant to contact you earlier, but I had so many delays on my new nineteen thousand square foot home— well, you know how it is, waiting for all those dreadful workers to show up and finish, and then having them redo their over-priced, sub-standard work." She looked Emily straight in the eye and said, "I'll wait. I'll have White tea, with honey," and promptly sat down on the sofa. She took out her compact and began touching up her lip color.

Emily wasn't sure she liked Ms. Goodman's attitude and sensed red flag number one with Ms. Goodman's description of her construction process to date. As it happened, Emily did have that kind of tea, as it was one she was quite fond of. She had been tempted to tell Ms. Goodman she only had *Black tea*, but though better of it. Beverly Park had very large, very expensive homes, yes, but most ranged from the prosaic to the garish. She had promised herself that Dar would be her last no-taste client with stacks of cash. Then again, she could get to know Ms. Goodman better and see if this potential client was worth designing for. Emily knew, more than anything, that the client's personality, good or bad or horrible, informs the project and sets the tone for the entire journey.

"Kimiko, take care of Ms. Goodman," Emily said as she went upstairs to extricate Toshi.

Candy's door was closed, but unlocked. Emily went inside and called out for Candy and Toshi. A delightful whiff of citrus welcomed her.

"Over here," Candy yelled in a cheery manner. Emily walked around the corner into the far end of the kitchen and saw Candy in her apron, arms filled with big slabs of cream cheese, standing over a large mixer. "Hey there," Candy said, surprised to see Emily. "How's that big-ticket, seventy-grand-fee art gallery project?" Candy asked. Emily was appalled at her crassness. There was no way Candy should know about Emily's business.

"What the...how did you...? Where's Toshi?" Emily asked looking around, not in any mood for small talk. Candy was in the middle of putting some touches on an elaborate, concoction of a cake, the components of which had been carefully laid out in place on the kitchen island, but not yet fully detailed and assembled. Emily thought it resembled an architectural model of a big wall. If there had been any kind of danger or trouble at Candy's earlier, it was not obvious now.

"Who?"

"Toshi, my computer tech," Emily said impatiently. This resulted in a blank stare from Candy Jones. "He responded to your demand and came up here a little while ago to fix your computer?" Emily pointed out, trying to jump-start Candy 's memory.

"Oh heck to anything," Candy said, "I forgot about him! Darn me. I didn't want the guy from the Minuteman group to see him here. You know, he's an immigrant and all, and I could have lost the account. It may not be seventy-grand, but it's a ton of money to me. So I pushed him in the shower and told him not to come out or I'd kill him. I wasn't serious about killing him, just about him staying put. Poor kid, I forgot to tell him he could go."

Emily, outraged once again, but with neither the time nor energy available to tell Candy off, stormed off to the bathroom and pulled a scared and embarrassed Toshi out of the shower. She dragged him past Candy, toward the front door.

"Hey, did you fix my computer?" Candy yelled as she followed them, just before the door slammed hard in her face. She stopped abruptly since she knew all too well what a slamming door meant in the world of baking. She ran back into the kitchen to discover the center portion of the cake slowly starting to reveal a deflection that was about to turn into a full-fledged sinkhole. Even worse, a gust of wind suddenly came through the window and pushed over a small section of the Wall Cake. Candy ran over to prevent the remaining parts of the structure from falling over in a domino effect. Not all a disaster, as a delicate twig with tiny leaves blew in. Determined to make lemonade out of a lemon, Candy decided she would use it as a model to make some edible trees to camouflage the sinkhole. The Wall Cake would still be ready for its unveiling at the upcoming Minuteman Ball.

"Hey," she yelled outside to the Latino tree trimmer, whom she was relieved wasn't there half an hour earlier when the Minuteman guy came by. "What kinds of trees are at the border?"

He carefully switched off his electric chain saw and held it to his side. He wiped his brow with his free arm.

"Which border," the tree trimmer asked, pushing his protective goggles up to sit on his forehead.

"Hello? Mexico?"

"I don't know, Senora. I'm not Mexican," the tree trimmer replied, bored from being constantly assumed by Americans to be Mexican. He placed his goggles back over his eyes and continued with his pruning. Candy shut the window and turned back to assess the damage. As she carefully began to examine every inch of the cake, the entire, laborious wall confection concoction collapsed right in front of her, sinking in on itself, oozing, spreading and gurgling, and finally not moving at all.

Back downstairs, Toshi was fast at work reformatting the computers, trying to forget about being imprisoned in a shower by a crazy woman and having to be pulled out of there by his boss, also a woman. He was embarrassed that Kimiko knew about it, but she had assured him she wouldn't mention it to another soul, and that anyone would have done the same thing if they had been similarly threatened. Toshi vowed to himself he would try to be more of a man. After all, Darren was the only other guy at the office, and he was out in the field most of the day. As experienced in the tech world as he was, his lack of experience in his personal life had been eating away at him lately. Maybe he should take this opportunity to stand up and beat his chest. He would learn how to handle this office, American Style. That is, until his parents would come, and decide if he should stay in America or if they should take him back to Japan. While he was determined to make a go of it in America on his own, he did find it constantly filled with challenges, few of which he welcomed. He wouldn't mind moving back with his parents. Their home was so much better than his shabby, roommate-filled apartment.

Emily was now thoroughly engaged in her meeting with Ms. Goodman, who was showing her lots of photos of her new super-sized mansion. Ms. Goodman had also mentioned that she was divorced, with two children in very expensive private schools, and looking for a man on J Date who could take on her entire lifestyle. Her ex, Mr. Goodman, was much older than she, but left her for a woman older than he. Ms. Goodman couldn't quite figure that one out, but it really didn't matter as she had gotten a huge settlement in the divorce and Mr. Goodman was quite the responsible fiscal when it came to his daughters.

Ms. Goodman was quite specific on her tastes and knew what she wanted. She seemed to have immersed herself in every aspect of the project. Emily listened intently to all the details, but assessing all the information at hand, things weren't quite adding up. Her experience and instinct kicked in and went into overdrive, enabling her to discern what, up until now, she couldn't quite put her finger on: Ms. Goodman was looking to *replace* a designer, or, more likely, to *threaten* her *existing* designer with a replacement. The latter was known in the business as Leveraging. In these cases, it was as pure and simple as you could get. It was all about neglect. *We have nothing to fear but fear of abandonment.*

"Whom are you working with now?" Emily asked.

Ms. Goodman had not been expecting that question and blushed. "Uh, well," Ms. Goodman said. "How did you know?"

"Well, let's just say I've been in this business a long time and leave it at that. Who's your designer and why isn't it working out?" Emily asked.

"Well, I have been working with Reese Witherspoon's designer."

"Editha?"

"Oh, do you know her?"

"I'm aware of her. The world of interior design isn't that big," Emily said. That Editha, again— flashing on the Pilates dust-up. She also recalled the charity event at which she and Editha were introduced; when Emily extended her hand to Editha, who then looked down her nose, and asked Emily to bring her a glass of Merlot.

"My project hasn't been getting the time or attention needed. I have paid a huge fee and thus far have received almost nothing in return. There was the initial meeting and one site visit from an assistant's assistant," Ms. Goodman said. "That was six months ago. And there was the issue of the bill she sent me for the ceremonial shovel that she *gave* me when we broke ground."

"I'm sorry to hear that," Emily said trying not to crack a smile. She knew that star-fucking designers like Editha took money from all kinds of clients. They had little follow-through with Non Stars, but got away with it because they were associated with Big Stars. Then, designers like Emily would have to clean up after them, with now-distrustful-of-the-designer type clients. If Ms. Goodman had been delusional enough to think she mattered as much as Reese Witherspoon to the Edithas of the world, then Emily didn't want her for a client.

"She's a very busy designer and considered top notch," Emily said. She had also lost out on a few projects to Top Designer Editha. Magazines clamored for said Top Designer's celebrity projects.

"Well, simply, she got famous first," Ms. Goodman said, "I must tell you, nothing in her portfolio comes close to yours. I looked over your website several times over the past six months. I wish I had met you earlier."

Emily could be a sucker. Most times, a comment like that would close the deal for Emily, schedule permitting or not. Budget permitting or not. For the first time that day, Emily smiled.

"Thank you. But I'm sure it will work out fine with Editha. Your project seems quite organized, and you seem very involved and hands on. I'm fast tracking a big project in Beverly Hills, and

I was just informed there is another one for the same client after that. It wouldn't be fair to you to say I could help you right now," Emily said, passing on the project before it had a chance to get to the offer stage.

"Well, I don't know what to say. I am not used to being refused," Ms. Goodman said as she got up, poised to protect her deflating ego. "I thought I would leave this meeting with a new designer aboard. What do I know? Thank you for your time." Emily walked Ms. Goodman to the door and shook her hand.

"Ms. Goodman, it was a pleasure meeting you. Thank you again for your kind words about my work. It means a lot to me."

"Not as much as I hoped," Ms Goodman said, leaving the office. As she walked to her Bentley, her chauffeur dutifully opened the rear passenger door.

Emily watched Ms. Goodman and her *Chanel* shoes slip into the back seat, wondering if she had made a big mistake in not pursuing Ms. Goodman. The car sat there for several minutes. Ms. Goodman appeared to be rifling through her bag.

Beth Konisberg pulled up and parked her brand new Compact Mercedes S.U.V. While she was walking toward the office, a voice from the Bentley called out. Beth turned around. It was only then she noticed the chauffer-driven, expensive car. The voice had come from the back tinted window as it rolled down.

"I think I left my photos in the office. Would you please ask Emily to see if they are on the sofa?" Ms. Goodman said, then the window rolled up. Beth thought this was doubly presumptuous on this woman's part, assuming that, A: she worked there and, B: she would fetch something for her on command. Beth stared at the entitled, clearly coddled, fashion plate, and then went into the office where Kimiko and Toshi were looking at the photos.

"Are those that woman's photos?" Beth asked. Kimiko nodded. Beth grabbed them from her and gave them the once-over. "Huge house. Nice house. New client? Can I work on this?"

"Not a new client, so no. But you can work on this. Enter these business cards in our database. Make sure everyone's information is current," Emily said, as she shoved a stack of business cards into Beth's hands and headed toward the back of the loft.

"Okay. But she's still out front. I'll bring these to her," Beth said, as she dropped the pile of cards on her desk and then took off outside. *Typing phone numbers and addresses*? That, along with *this is not the job I interviewed for*, were only two of the thoughts that bore through her mind at that moment.

As she approached the Bentley, the window silently glided down. Beth handed Ms. Goodman the photos, and added her own business card with the envelope. "I heard it didn't work out with Emily. Call me, I've downloaded all her sources."

Beth smugly waited for an answer, but then watched in disbelief as the window rose back up and the car gracefully motored away.

Back inside, a demoralized Beth carelessly sorted through the stack of cards, attempting to organize them by profession or product. A breeze came through an open window and blew several of them on to the floor.

SEVENTEEN

CANDY TRIED VERY HARD to wind down and deal calmly with her anxiety about the health department inspector's impending visit. She was certain he would shut her down. And even worse, she didn't even know when he would show up. Plus, Candy couldn't get past the caved-in Wall Cake, courtesy of that insensitive Emily Everheart when she rudely slammed the door. Thank goodness the Minuteman guy had seen her creation before it sank. The cake disaster was weighing heavily on Candy well into these late hours of the night. Not only would she have to compromise on the quality to meet the event deadline, she was just plain burned-out. For now, she just wanted to relax and watch a favorite movie on her new TV. She'd start fresh first thing tomorrow morning, hopefully inspired anew. She turned off the kitchen light and headed to the TV room.

Candy was asleep for most of the movie. The neighborhood had been particularly quiet that night— that was, until a hovering news helicopter broke the silence, awakening her. This caused Candy to raise the volume on the TV. After the overhead disruption came and went, Candy didn't return the volume to its previous level. The movie, *Once Upon a Time in the West*, was one of her favorites. She just loved the tough old cowboys and the shootouts. The buzzing flies added authenticity— she could feel that fly on her own face. The dead-on music that made up for the minimal dialogue, always made her weepy.

She was near the end of the movie when Jason Robards, who is in love with Claudia Cardinale, tells her to forget about loving Charles Bronson.

"Guys like that, they don't stick around," his character, Cheyenne, says with puppy dog, bedroom brown eyes and a sloppily bittersweet smile.

Then Charles Bronson comes in, packs up his things and says good-bye. The two-shot becomes a close up and bounces back and forth from Cheyenne in close-up to Harmonica in close-up from Jill's point of view to the rhythm of stirring score. Candy was so caught up in the scene, that she turned the volume even louder, as if to include herself in the moment. No matter how often she saw this scene, her heart always felt as though it were about to be ripped out of her chest. She knew both cowboys would leave the beautiful Jill. And sure enough, when Jason Robards leaves after Charles Bronson had left, she sobbed. And sobbed. Then Jason Robards dies from his gunshot wound and Charles Bronson puts the dead body on his horse and takes him back to Claudia Cardinale. The man she loves won't love her. The man that does love her is dead. The deeply moving music continued with its emotional pull and so she sobbed some more. Candy lit another cigarette and placed it in the already butt-filled ashtray by the heating vent, and let it smolder.

Emily was awakened by the loud music. There was cigarette smoke throughout her bedroom. She had been using earplugs since discovering the neighbor-generated, nightly noise pollution. The earplugs only helped up to a certain decibel level. After that threshold was breached, Emily would have to go upstairs because Candy would never answer her phone, as she couldn't hear it over all that noise. Or if she could hear it, she couldn't find it in her everyday, household mess. Emily made a mental note to install soundboard on her ceiling and to investigate redirecting the vent system. She had been putting off these drastic measures, but now realized she could wait no longer.

"Candy," Emily yelled like a maniac, as she pounded on Candy's door. "Turn down your TV. It's two a.m.!"

Even before she finished knocking and yelling the door flew open. A cloud of cigarette smoke billowed out the door greeting Emily.

"You must see this part of the movie. It's so sad," Candy said as she reached out for Emily and dragged her inside, hugging her tight. Candy was overcome with emotion, her body heaving so with each sob, violating Emily with each convulsion.

"I don't need to see it. I don't want to see it. I'm trying to get some sleep," Emily said, trying to push herself out of Candy's grasp. "Let go of me."

"Hey, it's the weekend. You don't have to get up tomorrow, I mean today," Candy said, while still sniffling from her sobbing, cigarette a-dangle between her teeth. Her bear hug on Emily loosened, but she didn't entirely let go.

"It's none of your business if I have to get up or not. You have no idea what my schedule is like," Emily said, as Candy dragged her towards the TV room. With her balance out of control from struggling with Candy, Emily stumbled over a large aluminum pot, causing it to crash into a metal cabinet. It clanged and reverberated as loud as a gong, adding to the chaos of noise anarchy.

Once in the TV room, Emily noticed, amid all the used tissues and the deafening sound, Candy's new plasma television and it's surround sound speakers, which were mounted on the wall, adjacent to the vent. It was a direct route for funneling sound and smoke right into Emily's bedroom.

"Here, watch this scene with me," Candy said as she queued the Movie On Demand to the right spot. "You'll be able to relate to Jill— both Cheyenne and Harmonica walk out, they just turn around and leave her cold!"

"Candy, shut up! Why can't you be normal? Get a date, go shopping or go out to dinner, get a hobby, anything! Turn the TV off or way down or I'll call the police. Stop torturing me. What did I ever do to you?" Emily screamed. Just then Emily recalled how she'd always paid attention to the home theater installers. She knew just how to control the situation. Emily walked over to the TV and removed the TV's programming card, killing Candy's signal. "What is wrong with you? Were you raised in a nuthouse?" Emily yelled as she stormed out.

Candy stared at Emily's back as she left. She couldn't grasp why her neighbor was always screaming at her.

Candy figured Emily was still lamenting her divorce. That must be the reason she was cranky all the time. Emily was just so miserable. And unfeeling. So unfeeling, she rejected Candy and her hug, and at a time when Candy needed her most. Furthermore, removing her cable card was not exactly extending the olive branch.

Not wanting an encounter with the police that night for several reasons, and feeling lusty from the emotion of the movie, Candy picked up a soft core adult novel and went to bed alone, but not lonely.

Back in Emily's bedroom, peace and quiet had returned. And then it evaporated. She had just cooled down and was about to fall back asleep when she heard the familiar sound of Candy Jones and the magic wand thrashing around. She had lived through Candy's self-sex escapades before and knew they wouldn't be over for another fifteen minutes.

This brought up again the idea of moving, although the concept didn't really appeal to Emily. She was just getting settled. After all, no matter where you went, there was always the risk of a neighbor-from-hell— although Candy was certainly President of that club. In the beginning she thought she could get Candy to behave better and to be more aware of her awful habits.

Emily got out of bed and went to the front office, where it would be quieter, to sleep on the sofa. There she wouldn't have to be reminded about her own currently sexless life. She noticed a business card on the floor that was partially hidden under the edge of the rug. Beth should have placed this in the card file, she thought. Picking it up, she noticed its peculiar graphic layout. It was obviously a do-it-yourself type of design printed on cheap stock. It was *because* it was so shoddy, that it piqued her curiosity, as most design related businesses had tasteful calling cards. She was curious which contact had such a poor marketing aesthetic. It read: "Tino Biscotti" and "Nino Biscotti" "Trainers-Bodyguards-Loans-Real Estate" with their cell phone and e-mail address. It also had their photos on the back— *super* tacky. Her memories of her evening on the town with Linda two nights ago were Cosmo-fuzzy-politan, yet she remembered the twins that Linda's agent, the obnoxious Judy Cleveland, had been talking with. She then recalled the waiter bringing her the card. What she didn't remember, or believe, was that she had actually kept it. The memory of that night, made her grunt aloud about what a zoo her life had become. The loss of Michael, from which she would never be the same, left her going through the motions of living each day, trying to find her place, her voice, without him.

She curled up on the sofa, inserted her earplugs and went back to sleep. She was able to fall into a badly needed, blissful state of unconsciousness, the lucid highlight of which was an erotic dream with Michael. She could feel him, experience him. They were back together and it was easy. Had it ever been that good? She touched him. He was real. Until—

Emily's eyes popped open. A jolt to her heart kicking into high gear, in sync with the pounding rhythm. She covered her ears, trying to mute the loud beating and grinding of Candy's high speed, noisy, industrial mixers that *were* drilling through her head. Instinctively she reached for Michael, but once her early morning eyes focused, she realized he wasn't there and panicked. All she could see were those twins' faces on the business card. She cast her gaze up at the ceiling and then back down at the card. A litany of Candy-caused grievances scrolled through her brain. The unwanted noise. The sabotaging. The pathological haircutting. The fake Yelp post. The backstabbing. The intimidating and disrupting of her staff. The insomniatic, insane, mind-fucking and hellish nights.

Riled and roiled, her blood boiled. It was at that very moment, as she felt a pop over her left eye and saw a brief spark of bright light, that something inside Emily Everheart snapped.

EIGHTEEN

OF COURSE THIS MEANS WAR. Nice guys finish last. Tweaked, and off-balance from last night, she knew she would have to send a serious message to Candy. The civil, tolerant approach had failed. It was now time for Emily to write the rules. Counteroffensive.

Reeling from neighbor-induced-sleeplessness, her thoughts did not seem abnormal or psychotic to her, but justified. Anyone of sound mind would agree with her, she thought, as she grabbed her running shoes for a Sunday run to work off her agitation. She loosened the shoestrings on her Nikes and slipped them on. She tied the laces up and stared at the uneven result. Emily briefly wrestled with herself that it would be just fine to run with one off-kilter bow.

The sun was peeking through some coastal clouds. It was going to be a magnificent day for a run— not too hot and just sunny enough. People were out walking and running, in small groups and large. A group of slender women, each with a large dog, ran by, followed then by a bunch of really old guys with winced expressions on their textured faces— a side effect from their aching knees. A multitude of new mothers, with one lone new dad, pushing prams trotted by, stopped and did deep knee bends together while holding on to their strollers for balance, chatting back and forth as they went up and down.

Once Emily got to the Fourth Street stairs, she stretched her calves to get ready to ascend the one hundred seventy five-step flight. An old, beer-bellied guy reeking of stale cigarettes and hard living was loosening up with leisurely hip rolls and motioned for her to go ahead of him. She waited for a break in the constant stream of hard-bodies climbing the stairs to take her place in the fast-moving traffic.

It was a tougher climb than usual keeping up with the pace of these regulars. A young woman talking on the phone by-passed her, as did Mr. Beer Belly, who took the stairs two at a time and fast. A middle-aged woman sporting a marathoner's body spoke in a measured rhythm into her phone mic, giving professional psychological counseling, as she walked down the steps backward.

The workout never got easier for Emily. Scaling the last flight she kept her gaze down as not to see how many more steps she had yet to conquer. The glittering mica chips danced about in the diamond shape border that married tread to riser. How appropriate, Emily thought, as she noticed how the entire detail was wedded to a burnished platinum bed, which somehow remained unsullied by the broken twigs, lifeless leaves and the colossal physical abuse.

Finished and at the top, on Adelaide Street, Emily counter-stretched her legs on the grass median. Still breathing hard, and feeling the impact after five stair circuits, she became aware of what sounded like a fight breaking out. She looked in the direction of the fuss, and saw two men in the street accosting another man inside a car, right in front of a construction site, about three houses down from where she was.

From what she could make out, the car had almost run over the men. The swarthy, young man wouldn't get out of the car, so the men road-raged him as he sat locked in his car, revving the gas as his only line of defense. After the big guys pummeled the silver *Tesla S* and left several fist-sized dents, the men punched each other in some brutal bromance-ritual. The driver, now pale and terrified, floored it, backing into the white city railing that straddled the west side of the street, changed gears, cut the wheel tight, ran the stop sign and was gone. The two men jogged away at an easy pace in the other direction, like it was no big thing. They turned a corner and disappeared from sight.

Emily couldn't believe her luck. She recognized the two men as the Twins from Hal's. Those were certainly the faces she had seen on the back of business card this morning. What a strange and fateful sign, she thought. She knew she could not turn down this opportunity. Even though she didn't know what it would lead to, she didn't care. She had to seize the moment.

She passed a plethora of city signage at the one intersection alone— Wrong Way, Stop, Do Not Enter— and took off after the two men, slowing as she passed the construction site (always the business woman hustling for a hot house) and read the only sign posted on the tarp covered chain link fence: Hand Dismantling, Demolition & Wrecking, with an 800 number. No signs of permit pending. No signs of contractor companies. Clearly, someone had wanted to wreck this historical beauty discreetly, without any pestering from pushy preservationists and aggressive anti-mansionistas. The remaining glorious old oak seemed to reach up to heaven in a last attempt to pray for a stay of execution, while the twisting cypresses trapped behind the shrouded fence, in foreseeing their impending fate, could not conceal their panic to escape.

Emily continued chasing after the men. As she ran down Adelaide and turned left on to Ocean Avenue, she could see them up ahead. She crossed the street and hid behind the bold red and yellow diagonally striped back end of a county fire truck and watched them some more. Behind her, a late model Maserati zipped up and abruptly parked, startling her. A very handsome young man strategically placed some 8x10 glossy headshots on his dashboard as he got out. He flashed a quick and confident smile and effortlessly jogged passed her, leaving a sublime musky, sweat-tinged trail in his wake which ignited an emotional blast, taking her back to the day Michael finally left. She paused as she felt the pang gnaw her gut, took a very deep breath and purged the pop-up memory from her brain.

Once at the park, just past San Vicente, the men settled down on the grass and started to stretch, with one standing over the other, applying some pressure with his foot on the other's back.

Emily cut deeper into the park on a decomposed granite path bordered with abundantly blooming periwinkle tinted *ceanothis* at every turn. She passed the heavy timbered picnic tables and glimpsed an Urban Fire and Rescue team practicing hillside rescue maneuvers. The span of ocean meeting the now-blue sky hung behind the rescuers as they heaved and hoed a gurney up the rugged hillside.

She slowed her pace to a walk and then stopped a few yards from the men and marked her territory. If she could hear what they were saying, she would have an excuse to jump in and start talking to them. Still just out of earshot, she moved a tad closer in their direction. She assumed a blatant and exaggerated downward dog with her backside towards the twins. She couldn't hear clearly what they were talking about, but she could tell she got their attention when she heard silence. Continuing, she rolled into a shoulder stand and spread her legs wide. Coming out of the position, she rolled to face their direction and, despite making eye contact, they kept talking and stretching. Finally she said, "That fucker got what he deserved. He almost ran me over yesterday. Thank you for kicking his ass."

"Yeah, sure thing," the larger one said. The smaller one nodded. They went back to their conversation.

"It was so right-on what you did to his car," Emily said, interrupting them. "I am so glad you taught him a lesson. In fact, I'd like to buy you two a drink sometime."

Tino stopped talking and gave Gino a look like they had a potential party girl in their midst, and another potential home-movie star. She was a bit old, but what the hell.

"We'd never allow a lady to pay our way," Gino said, acting all gentlemanly.

"That's right. How about tonight," Tino said.

"How about my place? Late. About midnight. You bring yourselves, I'll take care of the rest," Emily said, ultra friendly. "I've been divorced a while and it's about time I got back in the saddle."

"I'm John, this is Steve," Tino said.

"My name is Candy," Emily said, fire-eyed and guilt-free. She gave "John and Steve" Candy's address. Emily obviously wasn't using sound judgment in dealing with a couple of characters like the Biscotti boys. But the thought never entered her brain, since all she had on her mind was avenging what was once an aggravating situation that was now out of control. Every ounce of reason she had once held had been sucked out of her these past four weeks. Common sense had left the building.

The brothers agreed to come by at midnight.

Emily resumed her run. She ran past a park patrol clad in just-snug-enough tactical twill shorts, who was citing an over-muscled trainer for using *Pilates* resistance bands over large tree boughs. Navigating her way through boot campers, power walkers and the occasional blowup ball, she turned and ran down the California Incline taking the elevated crosswalk over Pacific Coast Highway to the beach. The ocean looked so refreshing, she knew if she didn't at least go in up to her knees now, it could be weeks before she would be able to, given the rapidly increasing pace of her schedule.

Once on the sand, she made her way to the ocean's edge, closed her eyes and listened to the cresting and the crashing of the waves as they pummeled the shore. She opened her eyes to a kiss of gentle spray, took off her shoes and headed into the water. It felt so good— instant relief from the now-searing sun. She waded in deeper and was up to her thighs when she heard a man's voice.

"Emily, is that you?"

Unable to place the voice, she turned and looked, shielding her eyes from the sun with her hand. There was a perfect male silhouette in front of her. It took a moment, but it came back to her. She beamed at her good fortune standing there in crisp white board shorts. The brilliant sunlight bounced off the surfboard tucked under his perfect arm.

"Chris?"

Chris and Emily walked and talked, sat on the beach, went into the water and got to know each other better. Any care in the world that Emily had up to now vanished. She was all-consumed by him. Nothing else mattered. They decided to have dinner together tonight. Chris would bring wine and salad parts. Emily would slow roast some salmon. They would have a nice, relaxing evening together. Emily would have sex with Chris. Mind-blowing, earth-shaking, noisy sex. So noisy, in fact, that her neighbor upstairs couldn't help but hear. Her neighbor would hear that when Emily had sex, she had it with a man, and not a hand-held device.

After going their separate ways, she scrolled through her mental list of tasks to do before Chris came over at seven. Stop at the market, review her work schedule, do a quick tidy-up of the place. Maybe they'd eat outside on the patio, so she should get some sexy lights that were all the rage now that the summer was here. And flowers, yes, some flowers to pull double duty for the night and for the client meeting tomorrow.

Back home, she put the groceries away and placed the fresh cut flowers in water. Quickly, she casually swagged a new strand of little lights over the patio table and sloppily wove the remaining string in and around a potted lemon tree. She stood back and analyzed her handiwork. She zipped back inside and returned with a classic glass hurricane and placed it in the center of the table. Nothing better than candlelight to set the night on fire.

She now needed to get her work out of the way. She planned to focus one hundred percent on Chris tonight, without any thoughts of her staff, clients or subs popping in and out of her head, torturing her at the wrong moment. Everything would be about her and Chris. Nothing and no one else would get in the way to ruin it.

Sitting down at her computer, she reviewed tomorrow's schedule: Darren would pick her up at 9 am and they would head out to Project Dar to meet with that idiot, trouble-making contractor, Frank Thorney. Then they would go across town to the Pacific Design Center to scout and pre-shop rugs and fabrics for Vivian Wyntor, then back to the office after lunch, where she would review the drawings and color boards Kimiko and Beth have been working on. After that, the new client, Ms. Wyntor— and she had confirmed Viv was one of the Forbes 400 Wyntors— was coming by to sign the agreement and give Emily a check. The last item on the schedule was a phone call with another new client, the Dufrenes, about their remodel. A few months back, when she had taken time off and was revising her luxury marketing tactics, Emily had purchased a mailing list from Lear Jets and Estates Magazine and had been sending out understated yet high quality calling cards extolling the value her services. The cards were individually addressed and said simply, *What would it take for you and I to have a meeting to discuss your properties?* The response was better than she had expected. Of course, she would still have to qualify anybody who approached her. While people on that mailing list appeared as if they were quite wealthy, they were often the opposite. But all she needed was one or two solid leads, every few years. The effort was proving fruitful. Dar had responded, and now, so had the Dufrenes.

Emily glanced around the loft. She should have bought more fresh flowers for the office. And the place appeared cluttered; that would be a turn off for the minimal and aloof Vivian Wyntor at the meeting tomorrow. Emily's research had revealed the differences in attitude and expectations from various wealth levels within the one percenters, from multi-millionaires, to billionaires (or B's) from old money to new money. She would have to touch up the office to appeal to Ms. Wyntor's comfort level by streamlining the everyday stuff and placing simple flowers at the entry— no filler, no colored vases, no mixing and matching colors and blooms.

She would need to have the staff organize tomorrow— which meant adding it to the task list now, so she wouldn't forget about it when rushing around in the morning.

Relocating to Beth's computer and bringing up the Monday morning "to do" list, Emily added the "reduce clutter" task to the schedule. She noticed a document on the desktop that had nothing to do with anything at EEID office. No time to look at it. She would talk to Beth tomorrow about using the computer for personal things. Emily continued to find Beth challenging to manage. Emily thought about letting her go, but then again maybe she would give it a little while longer.

Human nature, the part known as curiosity, caused Emily to revisit Beth's desktop document. Checking it out, she saw it was nothing more than a networking group agenda suggestion list for design firm employees. Some of the topics Beth Konisberg had brought up for discussion were:

1. *Dealing with an ADD/wishy-washy boss: how to organize your disorganized boss.*

2. *How to get paid what you are worth: incentives for racking up billable hours.*

Her blood starting to percolate, Emily stopped at that point and closed out the document. She went to the Monday schedule and added in first thing:

9 am: *Spontaneous employee review.*

Then she deleted it and wrote:

9 am: *Spontaneous employee firing.*

And then with one touch of the *LED Vierti dimmer,* she shut out the lights, shut out all thoughts of the office and Beth Konisberg for the rest of the evening.

Chris was on time and let himself in. She watched him intently as he walked towards her. She could tell by the look in his eyes he had been waiting for this moment as long as she had. Oh, it was going to be a really long evening. Yes. Long.

Dinner came off without a hitch. Everything was cooked and served to perfection. The salmon was just pink enough, and the salad divine. Chris was a man who knew his way around a kitchen (even helping with the dishes) and that was always a plus. Later that evening, after she and Chris had finished dinner, they were unwinding and sipping *eau de vie* on the patio. Her feet were in his lap, and he was massaging them. It was a blissful evening— the star jasmine was fragrant and the chic little string of naked lights cast a delicate, romantic glow. The sky was a deep black violet, endlessly still and peaceful.

"When can I see you again," Chris asked, as he rubbed her foot in a very nice place.

"You can see me anytime you want," Emily said with her eyes locking his. No need to be coy at her age, please. Her entire body was tingling. She wanted so badly to have sex with him; it was all she could do not to attack him. "Stay the night," she said as she gently pushed her foot onto his thigh. He gave her that gentle but perfect smile, as he bent over to kiss her feet. He said something, but she wasn't sure if she heard it right.

"I have to put my kids to bed tonight. I read them their bed-time stories."

He repeated himself. She *had* heard him correctly the first time.

Her first impulse was to throw him out on his ass, but she decided to not act on it this time around. Emily's second impulse was that of understanding while hyperventilating. "What time will you be done?"

"I'm done when they fall asleep. Sometimes it's earlier than other times. It's hard to predict."

"I thought were having such a nice time," she said.

"Oh, we are. We'll just have to continue it later. I'll come back in a couple of hours. For the night," he said. He set her feet aside and he got up.

"I'm already late," he said as he kissed her with a kiss that had some weight to it.

He saw himself out. Emily was too bummed out to get up. She sat there finishing her drink as the evening chill made itself known. She snuffed out the candle, watched the smoke twist and fight for its life and then die.

She dragged herself into the front office to switch on the out-side light for Chris, if and when he returned. She then grabbed the front trimmed edges of the silk drapery and yanked them shut. At the same instant, the porch light flickered and burned out. That's unpromising, she though bleakly.

To offset that hopeless energy, she lit a couple of votives and placed them at the front doormat to later welcome back Chris. The miniature glows passionately caressed and embraced the entryway.

She surveyed her bedroom. She had audaciously prepared it with beguiling linens, moody lighting, divinely scented oils— along with the cheeky panties on her ass.

What a waste, she thought as she snatched up a just-bought vintage copy of *The Supermale*[*] from the bedside table and chucked it over her shoulder. Her anticipation about his return visit disintegrated, now that the mood had been fractured. She hoped she would find it in herself to be nice to him when she saw him later. She lay down on the bed, stared up at the ceiling and dozed off.

Waking up to, yet again, thunderous noise, her first thought was to throw something at the ceiling to shut up that damn Candy. Then the noise increased, sounding as if someone were throwing things or being thrown around. Muffled voices bounced off the walls and flew around the room. There were at least two men. Candy was talking very fast, in a desperate, pleading way. Then there was some laughter from the men and even from Candy, which was followed by more thrashing around. The ruckus moved over to Candy's kitchen, so Emily got off the bed and tracked it. Pots and pans clanged and banged onto the floor forcing Emily to cover her ears. Large equipment and baking sheets were being knocked over. Then the clatter continued over to the stairwell, down the stairs and out the door.

Trailing the noise, Emily went to the front of the loft and peeked through the drapery. Although it was pitch dark with the front light out, she could make out the twisted shadowy forms of

---

[*] The Supermale by Alfred Jarry, 1902, exploits of a super cyclist's endurance and sexual athleticism.

two men carrying a large item, wrapped in what looked like the rug from Candy's T.V. room. The men hurriedly tossed the big and awkward object into the back of their car and took off without turning on their headlights.

The sudden lack of noise was deafening. Now, this different sound, one of quiet, one of stillness, was an unspoken truth of a probable mortality that Emily herself had caused.

Emily floated out of her body as she felt her heart clog, her throat and gut twist. The morning, which had been a long forgotten memory, returned to her, unmistakably clear. Sweat ran down her forehead. Sweat ran down her back. She shivered. Her breaths were short and fast. *There was no way I thought they would do something like this. They were supposed to show her a good time.* Her head was spinning with remorse, regret, guilt— all topped off with shock and disbelief. Steadying herself for whatever the inevitable blowback would be, she picked up the office phone and dialed 911. The line was busy. She tried again. Still busy. She looked up the non-emergency police number and dialed it. An outgoing message said to press one for English. Emily followed the instruction. Another outgoing message followed:

"Due to recent cutbacks, no one is available at this time to take your call. Please try your call again later."

Emily listened to the message again and hung up.

Just then she heard the sounds of someone trying to get in her front door. She didn't move as she watched the door handle joggle.

"Who's there?" she asked, trying to mask her fear.

"It's me, Chris," he said softly. She jerked the door open, grabbed him and held him hard.

"I wasn't gone that long," he said as he noticed her grasp.

"Long enough," she said quietly.

He looked at her. She had completely changed in a matter of a couple of hours.

Candy, not satisfied with the outcome of the last test pie, had been in the home stretch of re-working the key lime pie recipe for the latest version of her dessert book when the doorbell rang. She stopped writing a note in the manuscript margin and placed the pen on the counter. Still fixated on solving the problem of getting the meringue just airy enough, she opened the front door and was cuffed upside the head and knocked down. She looked up at two large men looking for someone named Candy. She told them that *she* was Candy.

"Watch her," the larger one said as he ran inside looking for *their* Candy, the hot-to-trotter they had met this morning. Candy got up and the smaller man of the two kicked her over again, then ran after his brother.

Candy pulled her phone from her pocket. By chance she hit the first speed dial number, which was Emily's. It went immediately into voicemail. She was about to leave a message but put down the phone because all she could think about was the delicate batter getting ruined by these bruisers. She followed them into the TV room where they threw books and pillows at each other. Candy held her own and chased the thugs into the kitchen, where she grabbed a saucepan and hit Gino in the head hard. Then she threw over a rolling cart, whacking Tino in the knee. Gino grabbed a large framed-photograph from the wall and said, "Where is *she*?" as he pointed at the photo. Then he went after Candy with it. Candy quickly grabbed a marble rolling pin in self-defense. But when she saw that Gino had dumped the perfectly peaked egg white mixture onto the floor she saw red and charged at him, her rolling pin leading the way. Just as Candy swung at him, she slipped in the now flat mixture, bumped her head on the stone pastry-dough rollout surface and hit the floor hard. She was out cold.

"What do we do now?" Gino asked, out of breath. He was still holding the framed photo of Emily and Michael.

"What do we always do?" Tino asked back at him. "Get the fuck out of here."

"What about her? She can ID us."

"We didn't do anything. She attacked us," Tino said to his stupid brother.

"I repeat, she can ID us. You know the cops are just waiting for us to trip up on something. You know what the immigration vibe is like now. We'll be deported and that isn't an option."

Tino looked at Candy. He stomped hard on her head, causing an excruciatingly eerie noise somewhere between a sharp crunch and a splintering crack.

"Now she can't ID us. Feel better?"

A disturbing gurgle spluttered out of Candy. Tino kicked the body square in the ribs.

"Now what do we do?" Gino whispered.

"Stop asking me that. Let's take her to go. We'll figure something out. Did you touch anything?"

"This photo," Gino said. Tino grabbed it and smashed it over his knee.

"Now wipe it off," he said, as he handed the broken frame to his brother.

"I'm hungry. Look at all those," Gino said, pointing to the various results, from curled over and droopy to stiff, shiny and opaque, all lined up on the counter in little ramekins.

"How about I buy you a candy bar once we are out of here," Tino said as he backhanded all the fluffy stuff off the counter. He wiped his hairy arm on a dishtowel. "Enough fucking around. Let's splitsky."

After they tossed Candy in the car, they pulled away at a snail's pace so not to draw any attention. Just as Tino started to speed up, a cyclist passed by, going in the direction of the loft, flashing his fingers in a motion for them to turn on their headlights.

The cyclist noticed the driver didn't respond to the gesture, but he didn't worry about it. He had a full evening ahead of him.

Emily clung to Chris. "What happened to you?" he asked. She backed away and looked up at him. Before she could manage to say anything, she threw up her slow-roasted salmon right there. It reeked.

Everything in a forty-eight inch radius got splattered, including Chris. Emily, horrified with herself, sobbed hysterically. Chris dragged her into the bathroom and guided her into the shower. He turned on a just-right mix of hot water and hosed them off. He then switched to cold water to snap Emily out of her hysterics.

"You have to tell me what happened," he said as he sprayed her with the hand held shower. She collapsed onto the shower floor. Chris shut off the valves. The pink tinged water eddied down the drain.

"Do I need to call someone?" he asked.

She shook her head no. She had no idea if she should confide in him. Should she call Linda? A galloping consumption of guilt ran her over as she lumped up inside.

"Breathe deeply, it will help you calm down," Chris said, standing behind her, as he toweled her off and wrapped her in her voluminous white terry robe. He reached around from behind her and tied the belt. "Let's get you to the bedroom. I'll make you some tea." He said softly in to her ear as he held her close.

An hour passed as he sat there with her. She managed to throw back a couple of Chris's bourbon enhanced magical tea concoctions. She had numbed some, only to become embarrassed. It was their first real time together and now she looked like shit and acted even worse. As much as she wanted to hide, she wanted him to stay even more.

"I'm sorry," she said when she had it in her to speak again, her warm glow now gradually returning.

"It's okay," he half-lied, staring at her, trying to read her body language, her face, her mind. Anything. He did not know her that well, but he knew Linda had a long history with her and that gave him some comfort. He had no idea if this was a typical evening drama with Emily, although he assumed it wasn't. Maybe it was hormones, he thought. She was about that age.

She lay there, propped up against the headboard, nestled under a bundle of blankets, her hair still wet and make-up smeary.

"I'm sorry I'm so messed up right now. Can you stay? I mean, just be here with me while I sleep," she said.

"Only if I can sleep next to you."

She flung back the blankets and he crawled in next to her in spoon. A little while later, all cozy and calm, she felt him against her backside. She was quite impressed as she backed into him. Yes, he can stay. Yes, he can maybe even move in.

He knew how not to attract interest while driving. He had turned on the headlights once they had cleared her neighborhood. He had counted for three seconds at each stop sign before slowly placing his foot on the gas pedal. After driving most of the night and taking the most circuitous, obscure route back to L.A., they had stopped to get something to eat at a 24 hour MacDonald's on Pacific Coast Highway in Malibu. They had pulled over and parked legally on the shoulder and had eaten in their car. They had finished eating an hour ago, but had decided to sit there to try to get some shut-eye. They both had been amped up on adrenaline for the past eight hours and were now crashing fast. Tino couldn't sleep, but Gino had nodded out quickly. Tino was relieved because now he could have some peace and think. He was sure their tracks were covered. He knew the chick— whatever her name was— would not be a problem anymore. Still, he wanted more quiet time, because you could never be too sure that the crime was perfect.

It was too early for most people to be up or out, so traffic was sparse. It would be a good time to go, Tino thought. He looked in the side view mirror. Clear. He looked in the rear view mirror. He looked ahead. He turned and looked behind them. It was a straight shot in both directions with at least a half-mile visibility each way. Not a car on the road. The only sound was the ocean's underscore bashing and booming in the background. He again checked the mirrors and the traffic. He waited a few seconds and checked again. He wanted to proceed with great caution— with the utmost caution— because Gino was slouched down in his seat sleeping soundly and Tino did not want to wake him. He didn't want to be bickering with Gino about shit because he needed to have his wits about him and not be distracted by minutia. He needed silence all around to re-trace their tracks from last night. He went over and over it in his head. He was sure they had left nothing behind. They purposely traveled without identification. He carefully pulled out and at just the right speed— not too fast, but not too slow. But before he even had the chance to accelerate, they were being pulled over.

Tino knew the drill. He rolled down the window and placed both hands on the steering wheel. The officer started talking before he got to the car window.

"You almost killed me," the young officer said. "You just pulled out in front of me without looking—" The officer became a bit startled when he saw Gino. "Oh, you're not alone." He quickly regained his composure. "Driver's license, registration, proof of insurance. Now," he said when he saw Gino stir and sit up.

"I looked. I'm sorry, Officer, I didn't see you," Tino pleaded, knowing not to disagree with this hyped-up officer who was obviously looking to pick a fight. He knew they were in trouble and was assessing his dwindling options.

"You just pulled out without looking. You recklessly pulled out and you almost killed me. I could cite you. I could bring you in. And you know— who would they believe? You? Or me? Huh? Who would they believe? You or me?"

"You. Officer, they would believe you," Nino said, in the same cadence of the young, clearly hopped-up on who-knows-what, deputy. The young officer was focused on badgering Tino, rather than seeing a driver's license.

"As I said, I could give you a ticket. I could take you in if I wanted to. You think you're the only one on the road? You know who they would believe. My word against yours. Who would they believe? You pulled out right in front of my car. Do you know how fast you were going?"

NINETEEN

THE BLARE OF THE ALARM hurt her head. She quickly shut it off. She wanted to sleep forever. There was a note on the pillow from Chris. She hadn't heard him leave. She could still smell him. She rolled onto the side of the bed where he had been until a little while ago, and read the note.

I'll call you today. I need to know that you are okay.

Today. Which made her realize that it's Monday. She grabbed her cell from the bedside table and turned it on. She could not remember what she had on her schedule for today. For some reason, her calendar did not come up. Maybe Toshi hadn't yet upgraded the software program. She made her way into the office to consult the master schedule.

Her calendar came up on the desktop monitor and her morning came back to her. Darren was picking her up first thing to go to the jobsite meeting with Frank Thorney, but she wanted to fire Beth first thing, basing it on all kinds of things insubordinate. Then there was the trip to look at rugs for the Wyntor project. There was also the huge task of updating her website, which Toshi was on top of, technically speaking. As was her style, she liked to give employees free reign to see what they could do on their own. Not surprisingly, she did need to have him revise it from his first pass, as it looked like an *Anime* style game, which would certainly not appeal to Emily's current client demographic. She had to guide the aesthetics, and that would take up some time.

She'd also have to start looking for someone to replace Beth. The project load was increasing and she needed more help. Maybe she could outsource another position— the office was becoming congested and she didn't have the time or money to find a bigger space. She made a note to review all the resumes and portfolios she had recently been emailed. The thought of her workload dominated her brain, leaving no room in it for her to fret about last night— the memory of which had surpassed denial and was well on its way to be stamped out of her consciousness.

After she had showered and dressed, and was putting on her makeup in the bathroom, she heard Beth shrieking. She went out to the office to see what had happened.

Beth was standing at the front door, holding her coffee cup, her face bizarrely contorted. She was pointing at something on the floor.

"What?" Emily said.

"There's pink puke on the floor and some of it's on my desk. I can't go in there. Clean it up. Don't you know I'm going to get sick if I have to go near it," she squawked.

"What are you talking about?" Emily asked.

"You know I can't come in with that sitting there."

"Well, I can't clean it up. I have things to do." Emily said.

Just then Darren, Kimiko and Toshi arrived. They easily maneuvered around the offending puddle and got to their stations without any trouble.

"Darren, clean that up," Beth said.

"You're not the boss of me. Besides, it matches the *canapé*,*" he said.

"Beth," Emily said, "Grow up. Interior design is not for the weak of heart. It's not Darren's job to clean it up. If you want it cleaned up, you can clean it." Emily switched her attention to her phone as it was alerting her to her messages. She turned her back to listen to them. The first one was from Ms. Goodman, the

---

* antique sofa

young-ish matron she met with a couple of weeks ago. Beth was still whining as Emily replayed the message to make sure what she heard was what she heard. She hung up before the other messages played back.

"Beth," Emily said, louder than usual.

"What?" Beth answered, a lot louder than usual.

"You are fired," Emily said. Kimiko, Toshi and Darren kept their noses in their work and didn't dare look away from their tasks.

"This is without warning. The puke— this is harassment," Beth said.

"Call it whatever you wish, but I call it breaching your confidentiality agreement, to start. How dare you offer Ms. Goodman my sources. The interior design world is not that big, and sooner or later everything gets back to me," Emily said.

Emily walked over to Beth's desk, went through the drawers, and took out a big can of hairspray. She held it out to Beth. "I think this is all of your personal items. Now go home," she said as she pushed Beth outside and closed the front door. Emily turned around to Darren and said, "Let's go, we have to meet Frank in thirty minutes. My car is parked out back." Darren grabbed his tote bag and followed her out the rear door.

Beth was fuming. Outraged at Ms. Goodman (Beth had only wanted to help!). Pissed off at Emily (the cow!). She started bawling and walked straight in to the ear-bud wearing mailman as he was making his way to Candy's mail slot.

On the way to Beverly Hills, Emily said to Darren, "I'm sorry you had to witness that. You have no idea of some of the things she was doing behind my back. And on company time. It's my own fault. I should have interviewed her more thoroughly. Her portfolio was really great and I thought she would make my life easier."

Darren could have gone on and on about Beth— her fanatical phobias and contemptible whining, but he decided not to. It wasn't his style. Besides, he was more concerned that they had an erratic contractor and a project load that was expanding by the day.

Once they got to Beverly Hills, they found a spot right in front— Doris Day style— unheard of for that area at that time of morning. Darren checked the meter hoping for a Jack Benny. An hour and forty minutes left! Two for two.

The jobsite was a mess and borderline hazardous. Clearly no one was in charge of this crew. A couple of rats scurried by Emily's feet and disappeared into the trash heap that should have been in the dumpster by now. No framing had gone up; *that* had been scheduled for last week. The metal studs lay stacked in the corner with construction crap all over them. Emily and Darren walked to the rear of the site where the contractor had set up his War Table. They looked around for Frank Thorney only to find a billy goat eating a set of plans that had been left half-hanging off the table. The billy goat ignored them. He dragged the plans onto the floor and kept eating, once or twice looking up at them while he chewed away. Emily's jaw dropped as she and Darren stared back at the goat.

"Is that what I think it is? I'll talk to Dar and have Frank relocated to another of his properties," Emily said to Darren. "This has got to stop or I'll have to bill him the *I-rate* surcharge." At that moment Frank came running towards them.

"Hey, why are you here? What's going on?" he asked.

"Frank, we had an appointment at ten to go over the low voltage plan," Emily said. "We get here. We find a filthy site *and* a billy goat in your office instead of you. What on earth is going on?"

"A sub owed me money so he gave me his pet goat until he could pay me. Isn't he sweet? I couldn't leave him in my truck and I didn't have time to take him home, either, because I got a callback for a homebuilding television show. So I had a lot on my mind. But hey, are you sure you told me we had a meeting?" Frank said, warily eyeing Emily and Darren.

"You told me it was on your calendar when I confirmed with you Friday, remember?" Darren said.

Neither Emily, nor Darren, wanted to pursue any kind of dialogue with him unless they had to. Rather than trying to have a conversation with Frank, and then be subjected to his dim witted ramblings, they continued the meeting pretending everyone present was of average intelligence.

Ignoring Frank's twitchiness, Darren opened up the revised set of low voltage plans and placed them on the desk where Frank's copy had been until the goat had them for his mid-morning snack. Frank's calendar was also there— with the appointment circled in red on it. Darren looked at the calendar, then at Frank, who was opening a beer.

"Don't look at me like that. What'd I do?" Frank said. Emily held her tongue, while Darren glared at Frank Thorney and, barely masking his irritation, began the meeting.

"Pay attention Frank. We have motorized window shades at the specified locations. As per the design, they will retract into a ceiling pocket. We have the wireless network, telephone system and audio system—"

"Those shades are all wrong," Frank blurted, as per his way. "We should have flowing drapery in the gallery to make it real sexy, you know what I mean, warm and inviting. Then we can paint some leaves on them with glitter—"

"Frank, just shut up," Emily erupted.

Surprisingly that was enough, to stop Frank's idiotic jabbering.

Having gotten the meeting back on track, they were able to go over the plans and make sure that Frank was current with all the changes. It wasn't easy, but they got through it.

"I could use a drink," Darren said, "In fact, after that meeting, I qualify to be over-served. Is your client serious about using this guy to see the project through?"

"That, he is," Emily said. "Now, don't you get cold feet on me. We can get through this. You know all projects are a bumpy ride."

"But why invite more trouble with someone like him? Your name is on this project. With Mr. Mimbo at the helm, your signature will be smeared."

"As long as I have some sway with my client, that will never happen," Emily said. "Let's pray he gets that television show and that he and that goat get out of our hair. I will be the last person standing on this project, not Frank Thorney."

They walked back to the car and headed over to the Pacific Design Center to look at the rugs Darren had the salesman set aside for the Wyntor project. Darren dropped Emily off while he went to find a parking place. Just as the doorman opened the door for Emily, her phone rang. The caller ID said Chris.

She answered. From inside the showroom, she stood facing the street as she talked. Yes, she was fine. She was sorry if she caused him any confusion, and would tell him what happened when they next got together. The sound of his voice left her in a near ecstatic state. She remembered how he put her to sleep. She remembered everything about it. "When can I see you?" she asked with one big thing on her mind. At that moment, and for no particular reason, she turned around and gazed across the rug showroom. Chris was saying something about checking his kid's calendar before he could make a date, but she didn't hear any of it. She took the phone away from her ear as she stared at something in the distance.

Emily's heart ripped in half when she saw him. And her. Michael and a woman were looking at rugs, looking as though they were a couple— not designer and client, not friends, but a couple. The woman was quite confident and assertive in her opinions and Michael didn't seem to have any problem allowing her to make the decisions. Michael looked dreamy. The woman was in great shape, not beautiful, but attractive *enough*. Emily turned her back so she wouldn't be seen.

She turned right into Darren. "I had to park on the top level. Sorry it took me so long. Did Joe show you the rugs?" All Emily could muster was a worn and threadbare headshake *no*.

"They're in the corner over there," Darren said as he pointed exactly where Michael and his female *friend* were.

Joe, the rug man, came over. "Please Emily, I show you the rugs now. Over here. Come with me."

Emily acted as if her phone were ringing, and pretended to answer. Not hearing the phone ring, Darren gave Emily a questioning look.

"Darren, you go with Joe. I've got to take this call. And then I need to go to the ladies room." She ran out to the lobby and found her way to the restroom before she could unravel anymore. She shut herself in a stall for a few minutes while she composed herself. She texted Darren: *Is that couple gone?* He replied instantly: *Who r u talking about? I'm the only one here.*

With the coast clear, Emily came out of the stall and checked her face in the mirror. Last night had taken its toll. Her usual softness was gone. She looked hard and haggard. She did not want Michael to see her looking like this, nor did she want to meet her replacement while possessing this out-of-sorts look. As she walked out, Michael's female companion walked in. Emily acted unruffled. It wasn't easy. Their eyes met for less than a second, but during that fleeting glimpse Emily noted a few things about the creature:

A very nice perfume floated in with her. Her shoes were expensive and S and M sexy. Her oversized purse was the "it" bag of the moment. She did have some lines in her face and her skin looked like it needed moisturizer: but an excellent make up application neutralized any further thoughts Emily had about this woman's wrinkles. No saggy jowls. Perhaps a mere hint of a nose job? DIY over-tweezed eyebrows. Aha! That's where she saves on money, Emily deduced. Great hair. A simple manicure with clear polish, but a couple of hangnails. The woman had smiled pleasantly at Emily as she passed her. Full lips. Nice, perfect white teeth. She was barely busty, slim hipped and with long delicate arms and legs. She knew how to assemble a wardrobe. She had an incredible shape. She moved with the grace of a dancer.

Well, I guess he's trying something different, Emily thought. She wanted to cry. He had been her husband, the one and only love of her life. Her wound had not yet healed. This Michael sighting had just opened it up wider. She could feel those high-end stilettos stabbing, ripping away at her heart, inflaming the emotions snarled within and blistering them into her head.

She kept her head down and continued to pretend she was on her cell as she zipped back into the rug showroom.

Out of the corner of her eye, she saw Michael waiting at the front entrance of the building. This wasn't the Michael she knew— just standing there, waiting patiently. He looked better than she remembered. But there was no way she was ready to say hi. She had refused any of his attempts to communicate since the divorce. She had further alienated him by pure isolation. Emily, now drawn into a toxic state of divorce darkness, could have just said hello. But at the moment, she was incapable.

While she had been reliving her divorce, she had gotten a few calls. Chris had left a voice mail. *"We got cut off. How is Wednesday night? Call me."* There were other messages, but she would listen to them later at the office.

She had to concentrate now— to get her mind off Michael. She had to look over the rugs and then select which ones would be sent over to the Wyntor residence. This was an integral part of getting the project rolling. These rugs would be the starting point for the interior palette that she had encouraged Ms. Wyntor to adopt. These rugs had to be great, but they could not upstage the respectable modern art collection that Ms. Wyntor had amassed through her series of divorces.

Joe was instructing two young Salvadorans to roll out the twenty by thirty-five foot rugs. With a rapid fire snapping of his fingers, the young men began rolling out several rugs. Darren and Emily viewed each rug from both ends. Joe would flip over a corner of each one to show the hand knotting.

"They look good. Send them over to the client," Emily said.

"Which ones?" Darren said, "There are ten. We only need three."

"You pick them. You know the direction we're going in," Emily said. She couldn't focus. She kept thinking about Michael and his perfect *femme* and her perfect *derrière*. Then she noticed the pile of rugs that her Ex and that woman had been looking at. Each one was uglier than the next. His new flame had not just no taste, but even worse, dreadful taste.

"How much are all these?" Darren asked Joe.

"Here is the price list. Each rug is on there," Joe said.

"Yikes. These are budget busters," Darren said. "Can you come down some?"

"Tell me exactly which ones you want," Joe said.

"These three," Darren said, pointing at the magnificent, antique, museum-quality trio.

"Those rugs are the finest of the lot. Answer on the price would be the same for anyone else," Joe said, "but for you and Emily, I'll give you a fantastic price if you take all ten rugs."

After they struck a deal for the three rugs, a young designer Emily had interviewed and did not hire, Cookie Jennings, entered the showroom. The young designer was escorting an elegant elderly Asian lady who emanated of old money. The designer was passionately bestowing the virtues of heirloom quality rugs to her client. Her client scoffed at the idea.

"I told you I want a more Western look. I don't want any of your Eastern style rugs. I can get these back home, much better quality for next to nothing. And remember, I don't want any *feng shui* either, you dumb girl."

"What an awful client," Emily said. She made eye contact with the young designer, who was flustered at having to try to rein in her despicable client in front of all these people.

"She should *Fire That Client*," Darren said.

"Maybe I should revisit my offer to her," Emily said, thinking she could use Cookie Jennings to replace Beth Konisberg. "Remind me later to see if we still have her information on file."

"We could put her on the Wyntor project and have her offload that cranky matron on us. The old gal just needs to be handled correctly," Darren said. "I can do that in my sleep."

"No, no, no. I am through with dreadful people," Emily said. "Don't let me break that rule."

They took the escalator to the third floor and went into a couple of different high-end showrooms in search of fabrics that would work with the rugs. After striking out at the first showroom, the next one had more to offer. Darren was going through the wings with Emily when the owner of the showroom came over to greet them. After discussing Emily's projects, the owner, Lorraine, showed them some of the newest fabrics and trimmings, which Emily agreed to consider. Lorraine also said that her cousin, Thomas, was moving to town from D.C. and would be looking for a design job. Emily said to have him get in touch. Lorraine placed the fabric samples in an elegant bag and handed it to Darren as they said good-bye. They had to get back to meet with Ms. Wyntor.

As they left the Design Center they walked out among various showroom employees, designers, sales reps and building workers towards the parking structure. The sound of footsteps bounced off the terrazzo flooring and mixed in with the din of worker-bee chatter. Emily wanted to be one of those carefree people right now— one of those people who didn't care about anything but the moment, one of those people who didn't look back. If only she could let Michael go. How much more time would that take? If she could stop thinking about Candy, why couldn't she just let Michael be a distant, yet fond memory? So far, it wasn't working out that way.

Back at the office, the neatly dressed, ordinary looking gentleman sat on the sofa. He did not allow himself to sit comfortably. He stood up promptly when Emily and Darren came in. He was holding two envelopes.

"Emily, Ms. Wyntor sent Ralph on her behalf," Kimiko said

"I was looking forward to seeing her. I hope everything is okay," Emily said.

"She didn't feel like getting dressed," Ralph said as he handed her the envelopes, tapping on the top one. "Open this first, please."

"I wish I'd have known she wasn't coming. I could have stopped by her place," Emily said to Ralph as she opened the first envelope. She smiled up at him, but he didn't respond. She noticed his bland expression and knew not to read anything into it. She had seen that look before on professional household help. She read the first letter from Vivian Wyntor:

"Thank you for the fabulous wine cellar ideas. I have decided to go in a different direction with a contractor who will do another design for much less. While it won't have the sophistication and cachet of yours, I am confident it will work for me. Please do not ask me to reconsider this matter. This is my final decision. Thank you, VW."

Emily looked at Ralph. His face was unreadable until he nodded toward the other envelope in her hand. She opened that envelope and removed its contents.

Ms. Wyntor had gone for Emily's "encouragement" for additional work. She looked at the check and made sure the amount was correct— it also included the balance of the fee for the now dead, wine cellar design. She saw that the check was signed. She flipped through the five-page agreement to see if Ms. Wyntor had crossed anything out— all clear. She checked the signature line on the last page.

"Everything appears in order. Thank you, Ralph, for bringing it by." Emily made a mental note to remember his name because she knew she would be dealing with him most of the time. Always be very nice to the help. Keep them close. Most of them have lots of clout.

"I'm so sorry about the wine cellar, Mrs. Everheart. It was a stellar design," Ralph said as his butler's bell text tone tolled. With one hand he proficiently pulled his reading glasses out of his breast pocket and with a flick of his wrist, he put them on. He silently read the text from his boss. He removed his readers and returned them to his pocket.

"There appears to be a condition I must add to the contract. What is the best way to do that?"

"Depends on the condition."

"The entire project must be done in complexion flattering tones," Ralph said.

"Pinks, salmons, corals. Got it. I'll have an addendum written up right now," Emily said.

"I'll wait outside," Ralph said as he turned and walked out, his wool suit too heavy for the heat. Once outside, he removed his jacket and lit a cigarette, leaned against the front wall and waited for the additional paperwork.

Next, they all participated in the weekly project status meeting. As the staff gathered around the conference table, Emily said, "Take the wine cellar off the board. Viv Wyntor is going with someone else for that."

There was a collective sigh of sadness. With no time to look back and dwell about what went wrong with the cellar, they got the ball rolling on setting up a program for the Wyntor residence. Then they covered the Gallery in detail— mostly construction notes to date. Darren was trying to tactfully stall an over-eager Dar from installing the art before they were ready for it.

Keiko then read off several e-mails they had received about e-design requests. Thus far, most of the inquiries had long, arduous scopes and wanted to pay anywhere between three hundred to one thousand dollars in design fees.

"Are you sure you are reading those correctly?" Emily asked.

Keiko nodded and showed the e-mails to Emily.

"I still can't believe it. Whom are we marketing to?" Emily said. "Make a note to research how to market this service to people who don't mind paying someone for working, please."

Lastly, Toshi demonstrated the website revisions. He was sure Emily would approve all of his changes. Beaming and proud, he opened up the site to present his creation.

Shimmering color wheel spins and electronic beats pulsed and winked as the home page slowly evolved, while an ethereal floral patterned mist retreated to the outer edges of the page.

"The primary palette is wrong. The colors are too bright. I know I said optimistic, but let's look at a tertiary palette. The format is still too slick. Who's going to want to see my project page after viewing this? It's pure sensory overload! Think Professional. Luxury. Beauty. Comfort. Zen. Visitors should be able to navigate with ease and not get caught up in the graphics," Emily said.

"What about a parallel universe site, for younger people? They have money and need interior designers, too. They like noise and action and cool stuff and like to blow through things just like this. And then keep the other, more formal one for the old...er...*more mature* people," Toshi said.

"Let's get *this* website finished. The one for us old folks," Emily said.

"Well, you know," Darren interjecting, "It's often the twenty-something assistants who locate the designers for their bosses."

"OK, then make it a tad younger. But I want formality and I don't want noise. I want money to be between the lines— obvious, but not too-in-your-face. And no anime gaming concept," Emily said.

The meeting had gone past closing time. As they were winding down, Kimiko and Toshi rushed to enter their billable hours on their time sheets. They had planned to get out of there on the early side because they were going to celebrate Kimiko's birthday with some friends, after work.

Darren organized his desk. He noticed a package sitting next to it and picked it up. "And what is this?"

"That's for the lady upstairs," Kimiko said. This caught Emily completely off-guard. She acted uninterested by picking up an unfinished crossword puzzle and studying the unsolved clues. The first clue read *"black, white and round."* Appalled at herself for being so brain-dead as not to have answered that simplest of all clues she let out a weary sigh.

"I have to get Cookie's information," she said at the end of the groan to no one in particular, brows scrunched as she penciled in O-R-E-O, ignoring Kimiko's answer to Darren. No one responded to Emily.

"Can you bring the package upstairs?" Darren asked Kimiko and Toshi, wondering why they didn't think of that on their own.

"The mailman said her door is open and she isn't there. He didn't want to leave it," Toshi said.

"We brought the package up there an hour ago," Kimiko said, "but we didn't want to leave it, either."

"Why not?" Darren asked, again dismayed that so many people needed to be instructed on how to handle the simplest tasks. He attributed it to their youth and their helicopter parents.

Kimiko and Toshi looked at each other, then gazed at their feet.

"Things are thrown around and the lights are on," Kimiko said.

"The TV is on. No sound though," Toshi said.

"The kitchen has a big mess. No one's home, the door is open and it's in a big disarray," Kimiko said.

"Doesn't matter. That's not your problem. You could have left it there. Next time tell the mailman to handle it," Darren said.

"I'm not going up there again," Kimiko said.

"Yeah, it's too weird," Toshi said.

Emily walked over and took the package. "Weird? Welcome to the world of Candy. I'll deal with the package. I'm sure everything's fine. You know she's not a tidy housekeeper," she said. We'll see you two in the morning. Have a nice evening— and happy birthday, Kimiko."

Kimiko and Toshi tried to take some comfort in Emily's calm reaction. They had been disturbed earlier when they saw the state of the upstairs loft. It looked like someone had been fighting for their life. When Toshi had been up there the first time, the energy *was* odd, but it had been upbeat. This last time though, the vibe was flat and soulless. Any life force that had once occupied the space was missing, obviously taken away with aggression. It's as if the walls held onto the screams. Kimiko and Toshi had noticed the weight of evil and despair on their shoulders when they went inside. This caused them to get out fast and not look back. Just having to explain their actions wrought extreme discomfort to their otherwise protected lives.

Later that evening, Emily stood at the base of Candy's stairs, holding the package between her elbow and her side. The return address read *The Judy Cleveland Agency*. She wondered why a big-time agent like Judy Cleveland would be communicating with Candy. There is no way Candy would have a book deal. There is no way Candy and Linda Sterling would have the same lit agent. Tempting as it was to open the package, she went upstairs with the sole purpose of placing the package in the entry. After all, Candy might return at any moment.

Standing at the entry door, Emily realized she had to walk into the loft in order to place the package on the entry console. She could see that lights were on, things were askew. It would be obvious to anyone that this wasn't just poor housekeeping. Something awful had happened here. A feeling of dread swept over Emily— the same feeling she had last night when it hit her what had occurred. What more did she need for it to sink in that she fucked up in an unforgivable way?

She left the package on the table and then backed out. Once out on the landing, she turned around and made a conscious decision to shut the door, pulling her sweater sleeve over her hand before grabbing the doorknob. With the door closed, Candy's world was now tightly sealed off from Emily's emotional reality. Yet her knees trembled as she made her way down the stairs.

TWENTY

I N THE COMING DAYS, Emily presented her design to another high society client.

"No, this is all wrong," the client, Len Dufrene, said to Emily. His wife was on the verge of tears after viewing the plans and renderings. He had been a schmuck for most of their marriage so, in return, his wife demanded, among other things, a replica of the *salle à manger* designed for Marie Antoinette for her Petit Trianon residence at Versailles. That original design was never realized in its time, but Mrs. Helen Dufrene did not let that stop her in proceeding with her very challenging and very expensive, "now you see it - now you don't" dining room.

"Well, we had to revise some of the details for engineering and City purposes. There was no getting around that. This is very close to the original design, but the challenges have made it even better. We have the best builder in Los Angeles on board and he's excited about getting started," Emily said, "We can work out the decorative aesthetic of rococo meeting modern sparseness to your satisfaction. If you approve these modifications, we can get a revised estimate. There have been several changes in the materials since our last estimate. And costs have gone up."

"I want to be able to operate it from the *Homeworks* system. Is that possible?" Len asked.

"Of course," Emily said, but deferred to the engineer for the absolute answer.

"Yes. There is also a manual system should there be a power failure," Bob, the structural engineer, said.

"But our agreement was for it to operate like the original design at Versailles," Mrs. Dufrene insisted. "With a pulley system. That's part of the charm."

"The integration with the *Homeworks* system is fine," Len Dufrene said to Emily and Bob, dismissing his wife's concerns.

"As long as I don't ever have to see the dining table again. This way we can sit down to dinner, dine and then leave without a care. And clean up for us will be one touch of the switch and the entire table vanishes," Helen Dufrene said.

"You have a staff of six to do all that. I still don't know why you want such a contraption," Len said.

"It's not that I *want* it, I *need* it. I cannot bear to see the table, or to see the help set or strike the table. I am haunted by the awful memories of this dining room. Even the mere idea of a dining room is distasteful to me ever since I saw you fucking the chandelier cleaning girl on the table in there. The mere sight of a uniform triggers horrible emotions," Helen Dufrene said.

Silence and stillness all around. It seemed as if no one was breathing.

"Well, you know how it is," Len said to Bob, man to man. He knew Bob would understand.

"No, I don't know how it is," Bob said, a devout monogamist.

The uncomfortable stillness continued, except for Emily's knee, trembling every few minutes since she had shut Candy's door that fateful night. Emily stood up to get the meeting back on track.

"Okay then, so I'll proceed with the revised cost estimate and have the builder pull the permits. Anything else?" Emily asked as she sat down.

"Emily, do you think we are over-designing this dining room?" Helen Dufrene asked. She had reached out across the table and placed her hand on Emily's arm, with a pleadingly sad look in her eyes. Emily quickly sized up the best way to assure Helen that this was the right way to proceed, given Len's half-assed support for the project. She didn't want to sanction them meeting halfway because she knew that the outcome would be compromised and she was sick of compromised projects. She also knew that Helen Dufrene was the ultimate decision maker on this project and Len was doing little more than acquiescing out of guilt. Yes, Helen had all the votes. She would play to Helen. She remained tactful.

"This is a fabulous and worthwhile design. If it were my home, I would do it. An added benefit is that none of your friends will have this feature in their homes. In fact, you will one-up everyone in L.A. And how often can one do that?" Emily said. She then changed her tone from decisive to empathetic and looked Helen right in the eye and said, "The removal of this painful visual intrusion will help you heal. Might I also suggest replacing that albatross of a table? Its history is obviously painful to you both. We can come up with something 18th century flourished that will be the proper fit."

Emily was damn sure that if Len had been banging the chandelier shine girl on it, she hadn't been the only one. A vision came to her of Len and faceless surrogates doing their thing on the silk velvet chairs. "And along that line, we should replace the chairs," she said, looking over to Len, who had cast his eyes downward and was rapidly turning pink.

"That's a great idea, Emily. You always know just what to do," Helen Dufrene said. She gave Emily's arm a fond squeeze.

"Do you know how much you'd like to spend on the table and chairs or should I come up with a cost?" Emily said.

"Well, don't go overboard. Let's say one hundred thousand," Helen said.

"Helen, that's excessive," Len protested.

Locking eyes with her husband, Helen added, "Of course that's *before* your fee, Emily."

Len shot a mean look to Emily, who acted as if she didn't notice the difference between that and his usual sour expression. Emily *knew* that Len *knew* that every dollar Helen spent toward their home would result in less money for his future divorce settlement, when he would go off into the sunset with the future girlfriend of his dreams— that type usually went *Yoko*. That, in her experience, was the reason most husbands balked at their wives spending. It had nothing to do with the cost of things. It had to do with love, or lack of it. There wasn't one good reason that Emily should be cost-conscious when it came to Len Dufrene. It was only fitting that Helen would be getting the dining room of her heart's desire and Emily would be profiting from providing her with one. And all compliments of Len's extra curricular activities and general worthlessness as a mate.

"We need at least 18 chairs. That adds up," Helen said, finally addressing Len. "I had no intention of replacing the set until I saw you and—"

Darren had had enough and coughed. "We'll have some designs to show you at our next meeting. It was great seeing you both again."

They all watched as Len and Helen Dufrene bickered all the way to their car. Bob the engineer rolled up his drawings. "I have no idea how you guys can do what you do. I seldom meet with the Clients and I prefer it that way. This room will be quite a challenge. I have no idea how the builder will make this happen. Maybe the Dufrenes should consider something simpler."

"You say that on every project we've worked on. And it always gets executed brilliantly," Emily said.

"I work with lots of designers and architects. Your designs are the only ones I lose sleep over. Can't you think about designing something less complicated? C'mon, a flying dining room?" Bob muttered as he walked out.

Emily had heard and ignored that complaint from all kinds of subs over the years. She could hand a sub the most off-the-rack product or banal design and they would still say it was too complicated but, nonetheless, do a magnificent job. This phenomenon was explained to her by a writer who said it was known, for men of a certain generation, as the *Scotty* syndrome. You know, how in Star Trek, Scotty would always make everything seem so complicated and dire, and then he would end up solving the problem and being the hero.

"That was an intense meeting," Darren said.

"I don't mind and you shouldn't either," Emily said to Darren, "The tough call is picking your allegiance in case they split up. The downside is that, usually, the despicable half will end up with most of the money. But I don't think that will be the case here."

"It just gets so personal," Darren said. "I would never air my dirty laundry in front of someone. But I got to hand it to you, you know just how to use it and get a positive result."

"Fact: This business brings out a lot of problems between people. I am a skilled listener and problem solver so they listen to me. Clients understand that I can enhance their lives. They trust my judgment," Emily said.

"So are you saying that an in-the-doghouse-philandering-husband had nothing to do with the added project scope today? That it is all about being a skilled listener and problem solver?" Darren asked.

"I'm saying that philandering husbands are great for business if one has the moxie to jump on it and not be timid about waving it in their faces. You have to understand that it's a way for them to get past a long simmering situation. Mrs. Dufrene said that in front of us on purpose. She wanted us to know. I couldn't, in good conscience, let that opportunity slip away and act like she never uttered those words.

"In the real world, most people don't want to put salt on the wound. They think the clients' personal lives aren't their business. But in interior design, peoples' lives are the heart of the business. You have to exploit it."

TWENTY-ONE

LATER THAT EVENING, as Emily drove off to meet Linda for dinner in Santa Monica Canyon, she got a text from Chris about him sleeping over tonight, after he put his kids to bed. He said he'd be by about eleven thirty. She replied OK. She wished her knee would stop trembling; maybe a couple of drinks with Linda and an evening with Chris would cure her nerves.

Emily became aware that a non-descript car was on her tail. Its sudden appearance in her rearview mirror had caught her by surprise. After two blocks, she made a right turn. The tailgater turned left. She felt some relief and wished she could laugh at herself for being so nervous. It struck her as odd that the sedan had come out of nowhere. The car had been on her home turf and she had been oblivious as to how long it had been tailgating her.

Just as she turned into the canyon, a flashing red light and a one-second siren blast startled her. She looked in her mirror, and to her dismay, it was a police car. She couldn't believe she was being pulled over.

The middle-aged cop shone a flashlight square in her face. He had big attitude, a bigger paunch and he meant business. He grilled her about where she lived and where she was going.

"Did I do anything wrong, officer?" Emily asked. She hadn't been pulled over in years, so she had no idea that one should never ask such a question. She could have sworn he said "shut up" in response and decided against asking him to repeat his answer. He continued talking while aiming the flashlight in her eyes, disconcerting her. What she did hear him say was that her taillights weren't "operative"—whatever that meant. He also berated her for texting while driving. Abruptly, he turned and walked back to his car. She tried to see what he was doing, but between the after-imaging spots in her eyes from the flashlight and his headlights beaming right in her face it was virtually impossible to see anything. The patrol car just sat there, its flashing lights illuminating Santa Monica Canyon.

A minute later, another officer appeared. He was holding out a PDA. "I need your signature, please," the younger, sweeter, officer said.

"A ticket! For what? I can't believe it," Emily said.

"No ticket, ma'am. I just need you to sign here," Officer Youngster, with the great body, said. He held the device steady for Emily and handed her the stylus. The print was too small for her to read without her reading glasses. She took the stylus and started to sign her name anyway.

"What am I signing if it's not a ticket?" Emily was curious.

"It's your sworn statement that we aren't, you know, harassing you," Officer Young, Sweet and Great Body said.

"*Are* you harassing me? You *did* come out of nowhere. What happens if I don't sign it?" Emily asked.

The cop gave her a blank stare. She could tell even in the darkness of the evening, his eyes were Paul Newman blue. "Please sign it, ma'am."

Reluctantly, she finished signing it and handed the device back to him. She wished she hadn't signed it, but by now she was completely addled. Had she had her wits about her, she would have thrown it back at him and his blue eyes. He looked at the PDA, looked at the patrol car, then back at Emily Everheart.

"We got a radio call from an unmarked. I don't know anything else, ma'am," Officer Young, Great Body-Sweet-Blonde-and-Blue-eyed shrugged. "Have a good evening."

As the patrol car pulled out from behind her and drove away, she noticed that both officers were staring straight ahead, grim expressions on their faces. *Really? Yelled at for texting?* As she sat there, one by one, the pieces started to fit together and click. She hadn't been texting just then. She had texted when she left her place, when she first spotted that tailgater. Was that the unmarked car the young cop was referring to? *Why are they fucking with me?*

Once at the Hungry Cat, and still slightly out-of-sorts, Emily made her way to the bar where Linda already had a table and was chatting it up with some people.

"Hey, I thought you'd forgot. It's not like you to be late," Linda said to Emily, "I'm celebrating. I have turned in the final draft. I am, again, officially a free woman as of four p.m. today."

"Wow, it's about time. That is great news. Sorry, but I just got pulled over, so I'm a tad preoccupied. Something about my taillights not working," Emily said.

Linda offered a sympathetic look and gave Emily a big hug. Linda looked relaxed and terrific.

"I'm sorry about your taillights. Let's put it behind us. These Lemon Drops are fantastic. You'll feel better very soon! I took the liberty of ordering one for you. I'm never having another Cosmo again," Linda said. Emily slumped down in the chair, clearly ready to throw back a few. Linda sat down with her as her drinking friends dispersed into other areas of the bar.

They clinked their drinks in a wordless toast. A server came by and tossed a couple of bar menus at them.

"What will you do with your days now that your project is finished?" Emily asked as she soaked up the bar room atmosphere.

"I'm already at work on my next project. No deadlines yet, just research."

"That was fast. What's the subject?"

"*Aftermarket Dating: The Upside.* I know Judy can sell it to a publisher in a second. It's a winner."

Emily almost spat out her drink as a distorted vision of the package to Candy from Judy Cleveland popped up front and center in her head, surreally obstructing her view of Linda.

"But your last book was all about date-bashing. Won't that be a conflict?" Emily said, as she sent her vision of the beat-up parcel packing.

"I know, I know. But really, since when has conflict stopped anyone from doing anything? There is no way any publisher will say no to this. It will be huge. It all started couple of weeks ago when I discovered, completely by chance, how to meet a lot of men without having to spend a lot of time and money to get dolled up. What would you say, if I told you that you'd never have to go to a bar or troll any of those internet dating services again in order to meet a man?" Linda asked.

"I'd say that I like bars. But, on the other hand, if you can nail that, you'll have yourself a best seller. So what's the secret to meeting men while looking like crap?" Emily asked.

"Two words. Pro. Sports." Linda said.

"That would be pure torture. We'd have to learn about football and hockey and such?" Emily said. The server appeared and they ordered several appetizers to share.

"It all started when my dermatologist told me to use sun block when I run— *and* wear a hat. I run about five times a week. You know I've been running for years. So a friend gave me a baseball cap with a logo on it. So I wore it out running. I couldn't figure out why all these men were smiling at me and trying to get my attention. On overcast days when I don't wear the cap, no such luck," Linda said, keeping her voice in hush tones.

"Which team was it and why are you whispering?"

"That's the hook, hence my whispering— I don't want anyone to steal my idea. So I'm going to wear all the different team hats over the next few months to see if the type of guy that I attract varies from team to team, sport to sport.

"I'm starting with football, then I'll go into baseball," Linda said as she looked around to make sure no one was eavesdropping on her brilliant idea. She noticed some guy two tables away looking at them, but he cast his eyes to his Blackberry when he saw her looking back at him. A young, hip couple squeezed their way into the table between Linda, Emily and the Blackberry man. Since they both were on cell phones, Linda wasn't concerned about them over hearing.

"I started with Green Bay. So far most of them appear to be civilized. There are few freaks, but no one too cheesy. My next step will be to talk to these guys. But— and this is another big part of the research— I don't approach them. They have to come up to me first. That's my rule," Linda said as she pulled a green and gold cap out of her purse and put it on, *"Ta-da*! See, it's not that special in and of itself and neither am I, but the combination works. I know I'm on to something here."

"What's that saying? The odds will be good that you'll meet some men, but the goods will be odd," Emily said, never having been much of a sports fan.

"Hey, don't rain on my parade. I'd like some positive support from you, my friend," Linda said.

"Hey, I'm here for you. And, even though I detest pro sports, your idea is a winner. I love it." Emily said.

The food arrived and was served by a different person than their original server so he had to ask who got what. The several small plates of varying shapes took up all the available tabletop. The couple seated next to them looked over at the array of dishes.

"The artichoke is my favorite," the female diner said to Linda, digressing from her cell phone conversation. Her male companion kept his phone close to his ear while he continued babbling on about back-ends and first dollar grosses.

Linda and Emily admired the simplicity of the artichoke presentation, which tasted as divine as it looked.

"Enough about that for now, other than I'm psyched about it. It opens up a whole new culture to me. By the way, how is it going with Chris?" Linda asked.

"I have been meaning to call you about him. I think it's really working out. He's really patient with me. I have to get used to the idea that everything revolves around his kids, even our sex life. And I do wish he were a bit more intellectual. We have nice evenings together, but we barely communicate. It's as if I have this other life after midnight with him, and by seven A.M., poof, I am back into reality."

"I believe the term is booty call. Still dreading reality. I thought you had passed that point of Magical Thinking," Linda said.

"Sometimes I think Magical Thinking is all I have. But, the projects keep me focused. I am grateful to be so busy. This is where I've wanted to be, professionally, for a long time. It just took forever and three lifetimes to get here."

"I know what you mean. I've learned that if you aren't on the kid-circuit or in Kabbalah, or AA, or Scientology, it's hard to network in any business. I find most people are comfortable in groups or, if the shoe fits, *sects*," Linda said as she nibbled on a mini-slider topped with a mouth-watering blue.

"I've toyed with the idea of joining something, and I'm still open to that, but my efforts are finally paying off. When I heard the size of my latest client's home and that they signed off on my fee, I am embarrassed to say, it was like someone was talking dirty to me," Emily said, as she finished her second Lemon Drop and chased it with an oyster.

"That's great that you're excited by your job. Not everyone can say that," Linda said.

"I'd rather have that feeling for Mich— I mean Chris. Never mind, I've had way too much to drink," Emily said.

"I told you these drinks were the best. This candied *fois gras* is yummy," Linda said. "It sounds like things are going good for you. Except, I guess, you'd rather be getting a thrill out of your love life than getting off about how much you'll make on a project. So, are you're saying the sex with Chris isn't good?"

"Oh, no— that's not the problem. Far from it. That's just fine. Believe me. I just wish I were in love with him they way I am— *was*— with Michael. All I want to do with Chris is fuck, cuddle and sleep. I could never discuss a book with him. Or travel. Or politics. Out of the sack he's just a regular guy. I'm use to exceptional."

At that moment, two more Lemon Drops arrived at their table. "Did we...?" Emily asked.

"I can't remember," Linda answered.

"We didn't order these," Emily said to the server.

"Those guys at the bar sent them over," the young actress-to-be said as she pointed to a couple of mid-western-stock guys at the bar who were smiling their way. One of the guys even gave them a thumbs-up.

"What on earth? Do we know them?" Emily said to Linda.

"That, my dear, is all about the hat. Did I not say I was on to something," Linda said as she pointed to her head.

They toasted again and Linda couldn't believe her eyes when Emily tossed back most of her drink.

"That's just what I needed," Emily said with a huge sigh. "Finally, I think I can shake this thing."

"That's out of left field. What thing?"

Emily picked at the last slider and tried to stifle a feeble snicker. She started to speak but fell into a giggling fit. She covered her face as her body convulsed with laughter.

"My plan backfired," Emily squeaked out between giggles.

Linda smiled. "Did I miss something here? What backfired?"

The room had become so noisy in the last hour that it was getting hard to have a conversation, even if you were sober.

"I'm such a dunce. It misfired. It didn't backfire. Oh crap, my head hurts," Emily said. She was starting to tilt to the side in her chair. Linda reached out to stop her from tipping over.

"We should have eaten more. Those drinks are too strong. We better go, but I don't think you should drive. I'll text Chris. He can bike here and then drive you home," Linda said, as she simultaneously signaled for the check and requested an espresso for her friend, all while texting Chris.

The server came over to confirm, "Okay, one espresso right away, and the check. By the way, if you are interested, there's a table of guys over in the dining room that want you to join them at—"

"Take off that fucking hat. Enough already! And no, I don't want to go. I can't let him see me like this again. And I have to tell you it wasn't my fault. She drove me to it— the banging in my head, the noise, her sheer dreadfulness. I thought it would be nothing more than a prank. I need to get this off my chest. I need to tell you. It wasn't my fault. You have to believe me."

This was so crazy, Linda couldn't gauge which of the two of them was drunker, but for the moment assumed it was Emily.

The server scampered off in search of an espresso. It wasn't often that people refused free drinks, especially at these prices.

By this time, the vodka-soaked giggle jag had become a waterfall of tears. Speech a-slur, Emily was an out of control drunk. People were starting to stare. The beefy guys at the bar got disgusted and turned their attention to another couple of gals. The hip couple seated next to Emily and Linda pivoted away from them so they could continue their phone calls, now being conducted during their dinner.

"You don't have to talk to each other on the phone for chrissake, you can talk to each other face to face," Emily said to the hip couple. The hip couple looked to Linda for some kind of explanation. Linda just shrugged. For whatever reason, the couple terminated their calls and seemed pleased to have rediscovered each other. Linda smiled awkwardly.

"What's so funny?" Emily shrieked at Linda.

"Not you. You're making a total ass of yourself," Linda said.

Upon having those words register, Emily hurled what was left of her Lemon Drop at Linda. In return, Linda hauled off and slapped Emily across the face.

The lone man with the Blackberry, two tables away, perked up when he noticed the spat between the women. Seeing that they asked for their check, he asked for his. He had barely touched his hamburger, but had managed to drink three beers.

Shortly after that, Emily and Linda were encouraged to leave by the male owner and a bouncer. Just as they got outside, Chris was approaching on his bike. Emily was starting to sober up by now and was appalled at her behavior. "I'm sorry. Go ahead and shoot me," she said to Linda Sterling, "Please don't say anything to Chris."

"What's going on? Are you okay?" Chris asked when reached them. He kissed Emily and brushed her hair off her forehead. His touch felt so good.

"Too much alcohol, too fast, not enough food to buffer it. Right, Linda?" Emily said, crinkling her nose, trying too hard to be cute.

Linda barely managed a smile but didn't say anything because, at that moment, she was speechless. She had known Emily for quite some time, although she hadn't seen too much of her lately because of the book deadline. It wasn't the alcohol; Emily was different now. There was no getting around it. Her friend was mentally breaking down in front of her eyes. The layers were deteriorating.

The valet brought the car around. Chris effortlessly placed his bike in the trunk and gave the valet seven bucks. Before they got in the car, Emily noticed the taillights on the car in front of them. "I want to check my taillights."

Linda walked behind the car. "Nothing wrong with them," Linda said as Chris opened the door for Emily.

The cop did say taillights. "Just wait a minute. Maybe they'll flicker," Emily said to Chris.

"Taillights working *bueno, senora*," the valet said.

"That's what we call good news," Linda said to Emily as she gave her an un-intimate hug and got in her own car.

It was obvious that Emily was disturbed by the fact that her taillights were in working order. She had deluded herself into thinking that it really was the reason she had been pulled over earlier. A duly sworn officer of the law told her so, not two and a half hours before.

TWENTY-TWO

IT WAS A DREAM of a sleep over. Part of a series of dreams he provided. He was consistent, no doubt about that. His skilled touch, his exceptional rhythm and his physical perfection— every time she couldn't believe her luck. And each time was different than the last. What woman would turn that down, she wondered. In return, he didn't ask for too much. He gave everything she needed for her sexual and emotional satisfaction. The mood all through the night had been soothing and erotic. Sex with him made her feel human again. Together they generated magic.

Not wanting to break the spell, Emily had opted against confiding in him about what happened that first night they spent together. Her soul was eroded enough and she wasn't ready to test his moral fiber. She needed to maintain the glorious status quo for as long as she could. She needed to be deserving of his sex, and was not going to risk losing it over some awful thing for which she was responsible.

Reluctantly, she rolled out of bed to get a move on. No headache— she had downed three aspirin and lots of water as soon as they got in last night. She made her way over to the full-length vintage, water-gilt finished dressing mirror and stood in front of it. She remembered the two of them in front of it, her watching as she went down on him.

She gazed in the direction of her reflection, her thoughts focused on the day ahead. Another jam-packed schedule. She remembered that the two new hires, Cookie Jennings and Thomas Renoir, were starting this morning. That meant Darren would have to go to the Wyntor residence to oversee the rug delivery and installation without her. Emily would stop by later to see how the rugs looked in place. More important, she would have to be the one to reassure Vivian Wyntor if she had any concerns. Darren could handle it, but when it came to huge expenditures, Emily preferred to give the client her undivided attention. Also, she reminded herself to tell Darren that Viv Wyntor *hated*—

She broke thought when she became aware of her image in the mirror. She was appalled. Upon further analysis, she tried hard to remember her last bikini wax and couldn't. Her line of vision crept up to her face and she realized her upper lip boasted more peach fuzz than she had seen in a long time. Her trademark eyebrows, left unattended too long, could now compete with those of Einstein.

She closed her eyes and slowly raised her arms just high enough to get a glimpse of her armpits. She opened her eyes for a blink and quickly brought her arms down and kept them tight to her sides. *How on earth?*

"Please, you can call me Cooks," Cookie Jennings told everyone after Emily had walked her and Thomas through the basics.

It had been an exhausting morning with the new crew members. It was non-stop introduction and review of office procedures and projects. She had forgotten how much work it was. No wonder even most small firms had full time managers. Emily went into her office to return some phone calls before anyone had any more questions about anything.

Cookie went over to her station and began working on the concept boards for the Wyntor Residence. She was delighted to find a very organized system, courtesy of her predecessor.

"I'm really looking forward to the next project status meeting," Thomas said as he went to his desk. His priority at the moment was to finish the *CAD* detailing for the flying dining room at the Dufrene Residence. Kimiko had gone as far as she could with the design. She even had Toshi help her, but it was all wrong— their revision was just too faux-futuristic.

Not only was Thomas Renoir's engineering skill a plus, but his degree and experience in industrial defense design would assist in more precise custom furniture designs, which were becoming more and more popular among the well-heeled client.

In her private office, Emily looked at her phone messages and scanned the project board. One of the messages was from Ms. Goodman, again. Perhaps, with the extra staff, she would have time to consider taking on Ms. Goodwin's project, who by now had gone from asking to pleading to begging. It wasn't even flattering anymore. Emily was grateful that Ms. Goodwin had alerted her to Beth's unethical behavior, but there had been way too many red flags at their meeting to even consider having her as a client. It wasn't her fault that Ms. Goodwin hired a star-fucking designer. *Don't these people get it?* Star-fucking designers only want the Stars— not the riffraff, not even the abundantly wealthy riffraff.

With the day's first mental rant out of the way, Emily focused more closely on the project board again— in particular, to see where the team was on a new private office for a rocket science think tank. It was a smaller project than she would normally take on; however, it offered the chance to design a sleek, ultramodern and exclusive space for an appreciative, high-powered and highly connected crowd of Pentagon Brass associates. She saw that the project's first review was scheduled for next week's status meeting and realized she hadn't yet assigned anyone to it. Thomas could design this with his eyes shut, she thought.

But more important, she had to make a waxing appointment straight away. She picked up her cell phone and speed dialed The Waxer. She must be seen as soon as possible. The Waxer had just received a cancellation for eleven p.m. tonight. Emily could come then or would have to wait for two weeks for the next available. Emily took the late night wax.

She hung up and, while adding the appointment to her calendar, her cell phone beeped, reminding her of unheard messages.

She hit the voicemail button and listened. Most of the messages she had already known about when people had also called the office. There remained one unheard message. She waited for it to start.

Just then there was a knock on her door.

"Come in," Emily said. She must have hit the end button. Either that or the phone cut out. She put the phone down.

"Someone is here to see you," Kimiko said.

TWENTY-THREE

"I DON'T HAVE an appointment with anyone," Emily said as she glanced at her calendar.

"Here," Kimiko said as she gave Emily a business card.

Emily looked it over. It said *"Detective Archie North, Santa Monica Police, Detective Bureau."* Behind her desk, from the waist up she might have appeared calm, but her knee jumped and started trembling again. It dawned on her that after drinking the three Lemon Drops last night her knee had stopped shaking. But that was then.

"What does he want?" Emily asked. As if Kimiko would know.

"I don't know," Kimiko said.

"Please tell him I'm not here," Emily said.

I already told them you were here. I'm very sorry," Kimiko said.

A long silence floated around the office. "Did you say "them?"

"Yes. There are two of them. The other one doesn't talk. Just looks around," Kimiko said.

"What's he looking at?"

"He looks up at the ceiling. I think he likes Cookie. He's watching her...work," Kimiko said.

"Is Cookie okay?"

"I don't think so," Kimiko said with a sad expression. "He's staring at her. Whatever she does, he stares."

"Okay. Tell them I am on the phone and I'll be out shortly," Emily said. She didn't want to talk to Detective Archie North and his staring colleague, but the last thing she wanted was to have Cookie get spooked by some potentially smarmy guy breathing down her neck and quit on her first day. She checked her face to make sure her teeth were clear of lipstick and that she otherwise looked presentable and professional. She rearranged her normally soft facial expression to a blank. She would be pleasant, polite and she would cooperate. She was glad her blouse was a tad tight around her breasts. She undid the top button to allow for the merest hint of skin, going with the notion that the two detectives were more likely than unlikely to be typically male in their attitude toward breasts.

She took a few slow, deep breaths. She looked around for something to bring with her so she could act preoccupied during the conversation. The Dufrene's line-item budget was on her desk. That would do. She walked out front and saw a tall man, who was broad across his chest and shoulders, looking at the finished project boards. He had on a long overcoat that was rumpled at the bottom. The other, Officer Ogler, was still watching Cookie's ass as Cookie assemble some other boards. The Ogler was well within anyone's comfort zone— he was tresp-ass-ing.

"Officer....North?" Emily asked in the direction of the tall man, as it was obvious to anyone that the other guy was the starer.

"That's, Detective North," he said, enunciating "Detective" while still looking at the boards. Then he turned around, revealing an aged, sun-baked face. His scruffy hair had a hint of blonde mixed in with the prevailing grey, suggesting some serious time in the surf. His gaze greeted her cleavage first, then bounced up to her face.

"And this is my partner, Detective De Meo." De Meo flashed a cheesy grin to Emily from Cookie's work area. Thus far Cooks seemed to be tolerating the intrusion, however the look on her face was sterner than usual.

"I'd like to ask you a few questions about your neighbor, Candy Jones."

If she knew anything from a lifetime of watching crime dramas and reading noir fiction, she knew to say as little as possible, and to say as little as possible while being as cooperative as possible.

"How can I help you?" Emily said with a gentle smile. She sat on Kimiko's desktop and crossed her legs, with the nervous knee on the bottom. The gesture worked. The trembling was smothered.

"When was the last time you saw Ms. Jones?"

Emily thought for a few seconds before she came up with her answer.

"I don't know," Emily said. She had an earnest look to accompany her response.

"Isn't that odd? That you don't know when you last saw her?"

"I don't think it odd. We're neighbors. We come. We go. Is something wrong?" Emily asked politely.

"We have reason to believe there's a problem. She hasn't been seen for two weeks. When was the last time you were at her place?" Detective North asked.

"Oh, gosh I really can't remember," Emily said as she glanced at the budget.

"So, I assume you've been there, you just can't remember the last time."

Oddly, *when you assume, you make an ass out of u and me,* popped into Emily's mind at that moment.

"Were you there anytime at all from midnight on Sunday, September 17th to midnight on Monday, September 18th?" Archie asked.

"I don't think so. No. I wasn't there."

Kimiko acted as if she were busy e-designing but was trying discreetly to make eye contact with Toshi, who was immersed in working on the website update. Kimiko was sure that Monday was the day the package arrived and that Emily said she would bring it upstairs herself. She remembered the date because it was her birthday, and she was late to her own party precisely because of that damn package.

"So to be clear, you weren't there on that Monday," Detective North said. Detective De Meo coughed a fake cough at Cookie's backside. Cookie ignored him and kept working.

"That's correct," Emily said, flipping through the pages of the budget as if she were looking for something in particular.

"Do you know a Beth Konisberg?" Detective North asked, changing tune.

"What?" This caught Emily by surprise. Detective Archie North turned to look out the window.

"Beth Konisberg," he repeated. He turned back to face Emily.

"She used to work here," Emily said, still wondering what Beth had to do with anything, but trying not to act too curious.

"When was the last time you saw her?" Det. North asked.

"I don't know, exactly. I had to let her go," Emily said.

"When was that?" As he spoke, Emily continued to look intently at the Dufrene's cost sheet. She really had to find that one particular line item.

"Sorry, when was what?" Emily said, doing her best to act distracted.

"When did you fire her?" Detective Archie North asked. He showed no sign of impatience. He would be there all day if need be.

"I'd have to check the calendar," Emily said as serious as she could, making it seem like a monumental task that would be difficult to accomplish, as she stalled for time.

"I can wait. Check your calendar."

Emily, unprepared for that response, walked over to the master calendar on Kimiko's desk. She was nervous. Her eyes couldn't stay focused on any day in particular. Then she saw what she already knew. Beth's last day had been that Monday morning two weeks ago. September eighteenth.

"Monday morning, September eighteenth, was her last," Emily said.

"As I understand it, you fired her Monday morning because she refused to clean up vomit in several places around this office," Detective North said. Detective De Meo snickered from Cookie's workstation.

"What?" *Don't fall for it. Don't take the bait.* "I fired her for a series of insubordination offenses, including violating her confidentiality agreement," Emily said, defensively and louder than her normal tone.

"And you," Emily said pointing to Detective De Meo, "Please stop breathing down her neck. She has work to do and you are a distraction."

"A distraction? That reminds me; maybe you can help. I've been distracted lately because I can't figure out how a package that the mailman delivered to you on Monday, got up to Ms. Jones's apartment?" Detective De Meo asked while he looked at Toshi who was trying to stay focused on the computer screen.

"I can't help you. I don't know. I just don't know," Emily said.

"Maybe one of your staff knows," De Meo said, still looking at Toshi, and then re-directing his stare to Kimiko.

There was no way in hell Emily could abide these weird detectives talking to her staff. She softened her face, smiled, then shrugged and went in for the schmooze.

"Look, we get a lot of packages here. Sometimes they are wrongly delivered to me instead of her and vice versa. It's not uncommon that someone here will bring a package up there," Emily said, trying to satisfy him so they'd leave, without giving up anything that could be used to hang her.

"You were close with Ms. Jones?" Det. Archie North asked.

"No. Not at all."

"To be clear, you weren't close with Candy Jones," Det. North rephrased.

"Correct," Emily said. *That's for damn sure.*

"Then tell us why she had framed photographs of you in her apartment. Tell us why your phone number was the last one she dialed, shortly after midnight. The evidence is obvious she was forcefully taken late that Sunday night. No one has seen or heard from her since," Detective De Meo said, walking toward her. "Are you aware she had an unregistered Uzi? Who was she afraid of?" He looked up at the ceiling again. Cookie left the area to go to the bathroom. She was verging on tears. Thomas went after her.

Emily knew they were messing with her. Candy never called her, wasn't living in fear of Emily. And there was no way Emily would ever give Candy a photo of herself— frame or no frame. Never!

"Here's my card. My direct dial is on it," Detective North said. "Please call me if you can recall anything that may be of help to us."

He walked over to her and grabbed the line item budget out of her hands, turned it right side up and gave it back to her along with his card.

"Now, maybe you can find what you were looking for," Detective North said. Emily stayed composed by ignoring North, but burned internally at her blatant gaffe.

"One more thing," Det. De Meo said as they were about to leave, "Why did you close Ms. Jones's front door when you dropped off the package?"

Blindsided. More like a sucker-punch. The momentary silence they heard was Emily trying to gather her thoughts once the words registered.

"I thought I told you, I wasn't there," Emily lied.

"We have a sworn statement from Beth Konisberg that's drastically different. She states that after you fired her Monday morning, at nine thirty a.m. she went upstairs to retrieve a red box of hers that Ms. Jones had borrowed. The door was open, Candy Jones wasn't there and the place was turned upside down.

"Furthermore, the postman gave us his statement that he left the package with your China girl here after he saw the condition of the place upstairs, at 10 am. He also states that the door was open. Now, the package that your China girl took delivery of is up there and the door is closed," Detective De Meo said. He winked at Kimiko, when he caught her throwing a mean glance at him.

Kimiko, horrified and insulted, almost burst into tears. *Your China girl?* She quickly sent Toshi an IM venting about the remark from the dumb cop: *bakatare. He speedily replied, concurring about the idiocy of the Detective. *He's a **kusai.*

"I must stop you right there," Emily said with a pleasant tone and earnest smile. She needed to get them off the subject of Sunday and Monday right now and, with any luck, forever.

"I do understand the urgency of all this. However, you're wasting your time with me. If you really need to know, I was with someone that night— Sunday. All night. Monday I was out most of the day."

"From when to when?" De Meo asked.

Just then Darren came bursting in the front door. He was clearly agitated, which was out of character for him.

"I have to bill you for *hazard pay*. I was placing the rugs just so, and Ms. Wyntor comes strolling into the room stark naked! She insisted on me showing her all the rugs! The delivery guys didn't care, but I did. Then she made me have lunch with her— still naked— at the poolside! Is my face still red? I need a big drink. I don't know if I'll ever fully recover."

Emily cringed. She had forgotten to tell him.

"Oh, I'm sorry! I meant to give you a heads up. She hates wearing clothes in the house. She walks around naked all the time. You can't take it personally," Emily said, getting queasy at the thought. Then she switched to a bigger concern. "Did she like the rugs?"

By this time, Darren had run into the back of the office to splash cold water on his red face. Opening the bathroom door, he was stopped in his tracks on seeing Thomas consoling Cookie. They exchanged the daily dramas to one another.

---

* bakatare: moron

**kusai: stinker

"Ma'am, please," Detective De Meo said trying to regain center stage. He wasn't about to let the questions stop.

"So who's that?" Det. North asked, waiving his hand at De Meo to hold on.

"He works for me," Emily said.

"Not him— the guy you were with on that Sunday night. And what time were you together?"

"As you can see, my staff is getting wound up. I'll walk you guys out and we can finish talking there," Emily said, as she didn't want her staff to hear any more. They had overheard too much already and were showing signs of breaking— the stress was getting to them all. She hadn't wanted to subject them to this, but she didn't want to be alone with the detectives either. So she had taken the risk and made the executive call that her staff would suffer, knowing she'd have to make it up to them.

Late morning traffic noise carried into the front yard, which dictated that they lean in close to one another in order to hear. In doing so, Emily noticed the unmistakable smell of herb on Det. North. She leaned in closer and discreetly sniffed again. There was no doubt; craggy old Detective North was cloaked in the aura of reefer.

"Look guys, I'm embarrassed to say, but the guy I was with that night is married. He's a good dad, just trying to raise his kids. It's not necessary to pursue him. I'll call you if I hear anything about Candy," Emily said. She walked between them toward their vehicle with De Meo staying close to her. He had the lingering, offensive smell of someone who didn't regularly wash his clothes.

Detectives North and De Meo got into their unmarked car. De Meo waved Emily over to his side. Reluctantly, she went; knowing what an asshole he was and how no good could come of her complying.

"Tell me something. I'm curious. You don't seem too concerned for someone whose only neighbor most likely got beaten to death and who knows what the fuck else. You didn't even ask us what happened to her," De Meo said, as he looked straight into her chest.

Two cars had honked their horns at each other while he spoke. Emily caught the snide comment from Detective Sleazeball, but then had immediately covered her ears on hearing the blare of the horns to act as if she couldn't have heard. These two repulsed her with their insinuations and their dirty smells. She backed away from their unmarked car and made a point of glaring at the honking cars. She gave a pathetic, limp-wristed waive as she turned to go back into the office and yelled, "I'll call you if anything comes up."

She bent down to pick up some flyers on the lawn and then stopped as it registered. *Unmarked car.* She turned to look at it, but they were gone. That realization made her uneasy. But she almost hyperventilated when she noticed the yellow crime scene tape across Candy's entry. That must have some significance—what exactly, she did not know.

"So what do you think?" De Meo asked North.

"It's hard to say," North said.

"She knows more than she's saying," De Meo said.

"Detective of the Obvious," North said.

"Then how can it be hard to say?"

"We've seen this before. Anything she can give us is probably useless. Just because someone gets nervous around us, you always think they're hiding something. They *do* hide things, just nothing we need to know about."

Just then North's phone rang. He answered it. He listened, said okay and hung up.

"Looks like we have a few new Jane Does to follow up on," North said. "Maybe one of 'em's our girl Candy. The closest one is at the Santa Monica Pier but the description is off. The other two came in from LAPD. They are too far away for us. We'll punt on them for now."

"Progress— whoop-de-fucking-doo. I just know Everheart is hiding something and I'll unmask it. Konisberg said she was evil. According to Konisberg's statement, 'Everheart hated her neighbor' and had said at one time 'she wished she would die' and I think, she even threatened to kill Jones. Konisberg also said 'Everheart needed more space for her business and wanted Candy's place'— that's it. She was driven by condo envy," De Meo said.

"Yeah, but everybody hates everybody these days. I don't put much credence in that— Konisberg is a disgruntled employee. I checked up on her as soon as she came in to report that something had happened to Candy Jones. She has worked for twenty firms over the past eighteen months. And besides, no one would kill anyone over a space that they could rent or buy anywhere. That's not motive enough. But I won't toss Everheart off our radar screen just yet—"

"Another thing, Konisberg found some bizarre photos of Ms. Jones in Everheart's office camera. When she asked Everheart if she wanted them downloaded, Everheart grabbed the camera away from her and downloaded the photos on her personal computer. Maybe some weird sexual shit between Jones and Everheart, eh?" De Meo said.

"I don't see it. That chick's into men," North said.

"Like you would know. I'm telling you Everheart is dirty. She will slink like shit all through this. Over and over. I'm telling you Everheart has a momentous role in this case. And, we'll talk to Mr. Married Fancy Pants, for sure," De Meo said.

"That's got to be the same guy Wiley clocked her with last night at the Hungry Cat. Did Wiley get a name?" Det. North asked his partner.

"Yes. But get this. The guy shows up on a bike," De Meo said.

"A motorcycle?"

"No. A bicycle. *And* he wears a helmet." They both snickered. "He drives Everheart's car back to her place where he stays until seven a.m. Wiley followed him to a yoga studio. His name is Chris Rouge."

"Chris Rouge. What's his story?" North said.

"Owns the studio. He lives with his wife and kids over the studio, but he stays over with Everheart about once a week. Looks like he can't afford a divorce."

"Maybe he just likes cheating," North said. "Did Wiley get the name of the woman who was with her earlier that night?"

"He did. Linda Sterling. Calls herself an author. A couple of self-help books. Widowed. An oldie but hottie," De Meo said as he looked at her photo.

Archie North rolled his eyes at the comment. "What else did his report say?"

"Packers fan. Ordered several appetizers. They were drinking Lemon Drops. Looks like the big note of the report is that towards the end of their dinner, they appeared to get into a catfight of sorts. He was out of earshot, but caught an eyeful. Oh, and get this, he also reported that she checked her taillights as they were departing. She seemed befuddled when the lights worked. So whatever the unit said to her, it stayed with her even through a few drinks."

"He used the word "befuddled?"

"Yeah, that's what he said. Why?"

"In talking to her today, the word befuddled would never come to mind. Nothing about that chick is befuddling. Not one thing. Doesn't sound like the same chick."

"Let me illuminate you. They were potted, Archie. Blotto, smashed, three sheets to the wind," De Meo said, "Drunk people are befuddled."

"Not this chick, so fuck your befuddled self. But taillights? That's lame. That's an old one. I can't believe it's still used."

"If you're a patrol, creativity is not your thing. They know one thing and they stick to it. Especially if it works," De Meo said.

Detective Joe De Meo looked at himself in the rearview mirror. "Did you notice how hot Everheart is for me? She couldn't take her eyes off of me. Not for one second. Did you see the way she scolded me? She was jealous that I was giving the cute, young thing my time. You know I'll nail her before this is over."

"Hey man, that reminds me. You've got to watch that harassment shit. That girl could have been my daughter, or yours. Dude, you almost crossed a line.

"And as far as Everheart? No, you've got it all wrong. Seriously, she was all over *me*. How could you even think she had it for you?" Detective North said as he stared over at De Meo, who was preening in the rearview again. "Dude, don't tell me you didn't see her cozying up to me? How could you have missed that?"

"Oh man, yourself. Get a grip. No, no, no. She was flashing me some skin, that's what she was doing. So shut the fuck up and commence toking or some other righteous shit," De Meo said as they sat in L.A. traffic and continued to argue over which one of them Emily Everheart was hot for.

TWENTY-FOUR

"**S**INCE YOU HAVEN'T BEEN IN for a while, see if your card needs updating," The Waxer said as she placed an oversized index card on the desk and handed a black linen robe to Emily.

The previous client was still in the changing room inspecting a first-time bikini wax.

"She'll be out in a minute. She's in shock. Her fiancé sent her in. She had no idea what he had requested," The Waxer whispered to Emily.

Finally, the woman emerged and The Waxer went to walk her out, through the back door. "Stop plucking. Let your eyebrows grow in. We can do a better shaping next time," The Waxer advised her new client.

Emily updated the information card and went into the changing room. The Waxer glanced at the card and filed it behind the previous client's card in the alphabetical file box.

The aging salon's buff colored walls had witnessed a variety of celebratory and civilian depilatories during its long history. The place was discreet— not fancy— and furnished modestly and tastefully. Not that any of that mattered because the shop had what it needed to endure and outlast all the copycats— it had *The Waxer*.

"What are we doing on you tonight, kid?" The Waxer asked.

Emily held her robe open. "The works," she said.

"Geez, kid. You're long overdue. Get on the table. Smoothie, right?"

"Sorry, I know I look like a guerilla."

"I prefer it. I have more to work with," The Waxer said as she inspected the area through a magnifying glass.

"I hate the grey. Let 'er rip."

Several waxed body parts later, Emily looked into the hand-held mirror as The Waxer described how best to arch the eyebrows. The Waxer embarked on sculpting away in detail at the area between Emily's eyelids and brow. It took wax, tweezers and scissors to shape the brows perfectly. They had been talking up a storm about interior design ideas— in particular, skin flattering lighting solutions. It was now well after midnight. Emily had been waiting for a good opportunity to bring up her situation, as she felt the need to unburden herself. She casually mentioned the visit from the detectives. She knew any topic of conversation with The Waxer would be confidential, since she had a long-standing stellar reputation, which wasn't easy to maintain in Beverly Hills.

"What did the cops want with you?" The Waxer asked as she combed the eyebrows into place, all the while examining her work through the magnifier.

"They wanted to know if I knew anything— like when was the last time I saw her," Emily said. "I wish I could have helped them, but I don't know anything about it." A voice inside Emily's head said "Bullshit."

"That's scary, kid. There're some crazy people out there doing crazy things. The client before you is in the District Attorney's office. She was telling me about a case she's working on with these two brothers who have been accused of date rape and other things. It's frightening."

Emily jerked. "What? Like what other things?"

"Hold still while I get this stray hair. I'm not exactly sure. I can call her if you really want to know," The Waxer said as she waxed on.

"That's okay. So the bad guys...are in jail?"

"I think that's where they'd be. Who raises this kind of people?"

Emily decided to let go of the topic. "These eyebrows look great. Did you do my nostrils?" Emily asked as she scrutinized her face in the mirror.

"Sure did," The Waxer said.

A mound of waxing strips had piled up in the trash basket. The Waxer cleaned off the table and said, "Nice to see you. It's been so long. Too bad about your neighbor. I wonder if she's related to that case?"

"I doubt it. That would be a huge coincidence. I don't believe in coincidences," Emily said.

De-fuzzed and feeling ounces lighter, Emily paid her bill and departed through the non-descript back door, the same path traveled by famous clients not wanting contact with anyone they didn't already know.

TWENTY-FIVE

"**W**HERE ARE WE on the Think Tank programming?" Emily asked Darren at the project status meeting, a week later. The entire staff was there, except Toshi, who was holding down the front office to cover for Kimiko, now pulling double duty as a designer and as chief note taker.

"We have our inspiration for our concept," Darren said.

"In one word?" Emily threw out.

"Drone," Darren tossed back to her as he pulled out a file filled with clippings and photographs of the latest drone. "This Terminator Drone is the ultimate in efficiency and will be our model for the entire interior. Thomas has worked on drone design, so his experience will be put to good use— Bravo, my man," he said as he nodded to Thomas. Everyone applauded.

Thomas turned on his laptop and launched into the overall detail starting with the space lay out. Next, he opened up the 3D sketch he was working on and explained the decorative features.

"All the soft furnishings will have a discreet zipper detail in the assembly— it's both rational and decorative. I designed a zipper for the Delta Missile, and we'll use that as the basis for this model," Thomas said. He circled the close up of the detail with a stylus and demonstrated how it would work. He then described how, when the detail was incorporated into the overall design of the furnishing, it would be all about function.

"You see, this is an example of the purity of good design. When a design works, you don't even know it's there. When it is broken, you'll know it's there because you'll hate it for the inconvenience," he said.

"Sleek. It's a great idea, but it could come off sterile. What do you see for the palette, Cooks?" Emily asked.

"Orange. It represents orange alert, the penultimate alert, with yellow being the secondary color, which, of course, is the alert just below orange. Based on the latest evidence-based color research, both are colors that inspire ideas that are conducive for tank-think," Cookie said as she showed the *Pantone* color cards, overlapping one another slightly as she laid them out on the table. "It goes without saying that there isn't any green in the space, unless you are talking in metaphor regarding sustainability."

"You are forgetting the atrium with the oasis," Darren said.

"That's not my department," Cooks said.

"Forgive me for jumping back in. I opted not to bring it up because even though it's visualized, it's still incubating. What I will do is give you an overview with my concept sketches. We'll have a dedicated area right here as an oasis," Thomas said, "with a lounge version of the furnishings flanked by two grand palm trees—"

"Whaaat? How many palm trees?" Emily interrupted.

"Two palm trees," Thomas and Darren said simultaneously. Emily stood up.

"Two palm trees do not make an oasis. It takes three palm trees at the minimum to constitute an oasis. You, of all people, should know that," Emily said with a tinge of disgust, as she redlined the plan with a third palm tree. Then a one hundred yard stare shot out from her eyes. The staff knew that look. She was about to drop a bombshell dead center in their meticulously planned soft presentation.

"Now, Cookie, that's a great point you brought up about green. Design this with the intent that we'll certify at, minimum, gold level. You'll have to put together a cost benefit analysis between a sustainable gold rating and a non-rating. I'll need to see the difference to be able to justify it to them. Every detail will need to be wrapped up before we meet with the clients. When will you have a full presentation and budget for me to review?" Emily asked Kimiko.

Silence. *Certification? Cost benefit analysis? Where did that come from? You want it when?*

"We're moving fast. We planned on two more weeks. We'll have to add those extra tasks in. Could take another week on top of the two. Do you want a real model or 3D CAD?" Kimiko said.

"Do both models." Emily didn't question the time frame, she just continued barking her thoughts.

"We need to tackle this from all points of view. These scientists are so detail-oriented that they will need to see this project from every angle of every dust particle. We have to strive for perfection in our communication with them. Leave no stone unturned. Okay. Where are we on the Dufrene project?"

Thomas started on the status of the Dufrene project, trying to keep up the momentum of the meeting. He wanted to wow Emily, because if he wowed her, the clients would be supremely wowed.

"Kimiko has come up with a fabulous dining chair design that has built-in capability to alter its seat height and back pitch, yet in a traditional design."

His eyes caught Emily's. "Our one word: Rub."

"A stretch, but appropriate," Emily said coldly.

"We have been going back and forth over the marquetry and sabots and can't agree on whether to use solid silver or burnished brass that looks like bronze," Thomas said as he placed two metal examples atop the waxed, black walnut stain sample for the chairs.

"The bronze. But use the *real* bronze, not brass," Emily said huffing loudly, causing Kimiko to look up as she scribbled a note about the metal detail.

"Noted. We'll carry the same bronze detail onto the tabletop. I've worked out all the technical aspects for the retractable floor and it will work like this," Thomas pivoted his laptop to show the staff, in 3D animation, the entire floor retracting back into a channel while the new dining room floor, dressed with table, chairs and fully laid out tabletop, rose up from a compartment below, then stopping once it reached the proper floor height and lastly, locking in place.

"*Et voilà!* A table fit for Marie Antoinette-Dufrene," Thomas said.

"If this doesn't get us a cover, I don't think anything will. I'm really blown away. Did the contractor re-price this yet?" Emily asked. Her awful mood was abating now that she saw the huge marketing potential in this most absurd dining room.

"We should have the new estimate by tomorrow," Darren said.

"We'll need a price on the chairs," Emily said.

"I'll work on that now that we've a decision on the metal detail," Darren said. "*Les Plus Beaux Meubles* is the best choice to make them, don't you think?"

"Certainly, but I don't like their attitude lately. We give them most of our upholstery and furniture fabrication, and I get treated like an incurable disease every time I go in there. It's ridiculous. We are the client but you'd never know it. Let's find another company. I can't give them anymore of our business," Emily said.

"They make everything for Editha," Kimiko said.

"Jett Jaimes, too. He just got the White House," Darren said.

"Therein lies the problem. There's no way I'd get the attention I need, even if I were to blow him and his entire staff. I may throw them a lot of business, but I'm not A-List. There has to be another fabrication house that can do this. I refuse to be a schmuck anymore," Emily said.

The staff looked at each other as if to say, "what's up with *her* today?" Kimiko had been taking copious notes and during the pause looked over what she had written. She assumed she must not have been paying close enough attention to the conversation and faulted herself for mistranslating. She simply couldn't make sense of what she had written down. *Incurable disease? Blow him and his entire staff?*

"We can try Cheri Cabrera's upholsterer. They're not far from here. If they make her furnishings, they have to know how to sew a straight line. She's extremely picky," Thomas said.

"Yes, I've heard of them. The upholstery cleaner has mentioned them to me. Please call them and ask if I can meet with them later today, about four p.m. I'll need a tour of their workroom to see some furniture samples," Emily said to Kimiko, who made the note.

"Kimiko, those are magnificent chairs you designed. The adjustable height is a great idea since Mr. Dufrene is not very tall. That's good, inclusive design," Emily said.

Kimiko knew that chairs designed in the West were made for people of average height or taller. Her own feet rarely touched the floor when she sat in a standard chair. To her it was a no-brainer to make furnishings that would accommodate *all* of the population instead of *some* of it.

"Thank you very much," Kimiko said. Somehow her mind kept going back to Emily lying to the Detectives last week. Maybe, she told herself, it was her own memory that was in error. But deep down inside she knew that wasn't the case. Her boss did lie.

"What else do we need to cover?" Emily asked.

"Vivian Wyntor likes all the rugs. She loves the fact that they don't compete with her art collection. And she *really* loves the fact that when she sits on them, they don't scratch her," Darren said, turning beet red as he read his project notes. Everyone in the room smiled.

"She has given me a laundry list of mini-projects. Here it is: She now wants us to completely re-do her master bathroom. Recover all her furniture. She needs new sheets for her bed. She wants a new lamp on her desk in her home office. A new plasma in her home theatre. And the custom wine cellar her builder put in is making loud noises—"

"That wasn't us. She didn't like our design or our estimate. She can call her builder to fix it," Emily said.

"I think she's feeling guilty. She did save ten grand by going with the guy. And she doesn't even drink wine," Darren said.

"I don't care if she doesn't drink it. She collects it and she treats it like art, so it needs the best storage possible. I warned her it was not apples to apples. Our design was so much better and she knew it, but she still went with him. Another do-it-yourself project that we have to clean up after," Emily said.

"Look at it this way. Sometimes they try to save money when they don't really care about a certain area. I think it's so they can spend more somewhere else in the house," Darren said.

"I know *that*," Emily said. "We'll chalk it up as part of our Value Added Extra Service and take care of it. But, we'll have to let her know it is a favor. Then we'll use it to turn over all the furniture completely instead of just recovering.

"So let's add those tasks to the Wyntor rotation. Cooks, set up an appointment to meet with the Portugeuse linen bedding rep to see the latest line. You're going to have to take over the project visits from Darren. Can you handle that?" Emily said, hoping Cookie wouldn't be bothered by a client who was really quite polite, lovely, and easy going, albeit naked most of the time.

Cookie evinced a look of horror on her face, but quickly masked it. "I'll try anything once," she said. "What's a little skin?"

"Nothing, if it's in good condition. But this, it's crumpled and crinkly— quite unaesthetic. You are such a good sport," Darren whispered as he leaned in to Cookie's ear. Cookie's jaw dropped as she visualized the saggy flesh.

"Is that it for the projects?" Emily asked, looking at her watch. She had to meet the lighting specialist shortly.

"One more. Project Dar Gallery," Darren said. "It's really moving along. We are sampling the custom purple mixes for the walls and I don't think any of them are quite right. You'll need to go down there to see the tones yourself. They are nothing like our samples. I think they may be substituting the brand we've specified, although they tell me they are not."

"Is Frank getting involved with the paint?" Emily asked warily.

"He says he knows color," Darren said.

"I bet he's telling the paint crew to use a cheaper paint. Remind me to check it out to see their results," Emily said. The thought of Frank Thorney made her blood pressure spike.

"I stress, this needs your immediate attention. We can't trust him on getting involved with something as important as color," Darren pleaded.

"All right, all right, now shut up about it. I get it," Emily sharply snapped. The remark was not out of character for most bosses, but it was out of character for Emily. Everyone looked at her. Darren cleared his throat.

"Continuing on, the art displays are about finished at the manufacturers. You will need to approve them in person before they are shipped to the finisher. The partially dropped ceiling still has to go in, as does the low voltage trim," Darren said.

"Who's in charge of troubleshooting the ceiling conditions?" Emily asked.

"Frank Thorney," Darren said. Emily dropped her pen on the table and crossed her arms. She let out an exaggerated sigh.

"You, me and Thomas go there first thing tomorrow. I don't want Frank troubleshooting anything. He'll draw out the process by making it too complicated. He over-thinks and wrong-thinks. That ceiling connection is designed to be trouble-free. It should be something relatively minor to deal with. Put it on the schedule for first thing," Emily said. Kimiko scribbled away.

"Lastly," Darren said, "Ms. Goodman has left several messages. Something about a magazine editor."

"If she thinks she can get my attention by enticing me with a potential magazine spread, she's out of her mind. I have told her repeatedly we just can't take her on right now. Dar has another large project that will be coming in. I don't know when, but it will happen, and he gets our priority," Emily said.

"You've told us that, but I'm not sure you have told her that, at least not recently. We can put her on a waiting list. When Dufrene is done we'll have an opening," Darren said. He did not like the idea of losing a good project. "Or do you want to refer her to someone?"

"Whose company is this?" she snapped. "I don't want to work with her. Nor am I certain I want to refer her. But let me think about that before we officially pass." Emily stood up to signal the meeting was over. "I'll be in my office. Send in the lighting rep when he gets here." As she walked away, she turned on her phone and it beeped, indicating she had new messages. She stumbled on the way out, even though there was nothing on the floor to stumble over.

"Crashing hormones?" Darren said to Thomas and Cooks.

"May God help us all," Thomas said.

"I guess you queens would know," Cookie said with a laugh as she tugged on her nipped and tailored shift. She headed toward her workstation.

"Very funny, Ms. Orange Alert," Thomas said to her wake.

"Remind me to remind Emily of our site visit to see the paint colors at the Gallery tomorrow," Darren said to Kimiko and Thomas.

"I have put it in her schedule already," Kimiko said.

"Please, please, please, remind her in person at the end of the day and in the morning as well. I will too," Darren said. "She is way off in a weird way today. She's distracted. She has to be on top of her game at that meeting tomorrow. She can't forget."

"Hey, I'm digressing here, but did I miss something about going for a certification on the Think Tank? Is that coming from the client?" Thomas asked Darren.

"You did not miss anything. I have no idea where that came from. This is the first any of us heard about it. That'll blow any budget off the planet. We'll have to scramble. I do hope your zippers are recyclable," Darren said.

"My zippers have a very long life cycle and eventually bio degrade," Thomas said.

"Well, what rationale will we have for redecorating in the future? Can't you give the zippers a shorter life cycle?"

"Oh, I can do anything with my zippers," Thomas said as he winked at Darren.

TWENTY-SIX

EMILY WAS LISTENING to some of her messages when Kimiko walked the LED lighting designer into her office. Chris had called, confirming he would see her later tonight. She played his message a few times, indulging herself in hearing his voice over and over. It was a needed distraction right now. As she thought about Chris, Emily remembered that Linda had left a message for her to call as soon as possible. Emily would do that right after the LED guy left.

"Look Brad, I'll be honest with you. I would like to specify the new light-emitting wall finish for the gallery, but I'm uncomfortable using it when there isn't much research out there to support the technology. Even the few times I have used LED lighting the result wasn't satisfactory. They neither performed well, nor lasted. Plus, I never get any support. No one can tell me anything except that LED lighting is the future and the technology is improving. I'm getting cold feet. I'm now thinking I shouldn't take the chance," Emily carped.

"I'm sorry," Brad said empathetically, "I know it's frustrating, but any glitch will be resolved by the time we install. What's great about it is that, the light emitting wall finish has a chemical coating that won't alter your purple wall color. You'll have natural daylight around the clock. Your client will love the savings. The entire thing takes only about five volts to run. It'll last for decades. If the system doesn't perform, you have my word that I'll stand by it. This is a no-brainer, Emily. What is not to like?

"Now on a residential note, let me show you a prototype of something new we are doing. We're marrying old and new ideas, so the problems are practically non-existent."

He pulled out a twelve-inch section of a round metal bar. The bar had a reveal running lengthwise with an LED light strip barely visible. He plugged it in. It lit up and he held it out for her to see.

"Don't tell me, I can light my clothes while they hang in the wardrobe? Okay, you got me. This one I can get my head around," Emily said, smitten with the product. "But couldn't I use a rope light instead? Or a mini-halogen strip?"

"Those will soon be obsolete and these won't burn your clothes. You'll be able to see much better. Face it, none of us is getting any younger. We will need all the illumination we can get," Brad said.

"I'll give it some thought. Any product I specify has to work. What happens if one lamp burns out? How do I replace it?"

"You'd have to take the whole thing apart, replace the entire strip and re-install."

"Could a homeowner's assistant do that or is it something an electrician would have to do?"

"Electrician."

"Okay, end of discussion. Thanks for stopping by. Can you see yourself out?"

Brad gathered up his things. As wealthy as her clients are, if they're spending money on something, they expect it to work. Even more than the 99 percenters, the wealthy hate it when things break down. Their staffs have better things to do than coordinate repairs of overpriced items.

"I'll call you in a couple of weeks to follow up," Brad said as he walked out. Emily sat behind her desk. From that point of view her gaze was drawn as if by a magnetic force to the way Brad's pants hugged his glorious gluteus maximus. She immediately thought of Chris.

"Close the door," she yelled after Brad's backside.

Emily was more than eager to call Chris back, even though she didn't have to. She had become obsessed with their nights together. The mere sound of his voice intoxicated her. He always left her craving more. Lost in those thoughts, she couldn't resist and she called him. A woman answered his *cell phone*. At the same time, her phone beeped, distracting her. The readout said it was another message from Linda Sterling.

"Hello? Hello?" the young woman's voice said from Chris's phone.

"I must have dialed the wrong number," Emily said, not knowing what else to say.

"No, you didn't? Hang on? Chris? The phone?" the woman called out, sounding even younger with a low-end, snappy valley twang.

Just then, Darren opened the door, just enough to poke his head in. "It's time to go to check out the new upholstery house. They're staying open late to wait for us," he said.

Emily nodded and signaled she'd be there in a minute. Chris was taking forever to come to the phone.

"Hello," Chris said just as Emily was about to hang up.

"Was that your daughter?" Emily asked. No time for small talk— besides, who else would answer his phone?

"No, that was a client," Chris said. "I couldn't get to my phone in time."

A client answering *his* phone? How inappropriate.

"What are you doing?" Emily asked.

"I'm teaching them yoga massage," he said. Emily knew everything about his yoga massages, including the get-naked-maximization techniques. And so she wasn't ready to hang up just yet.

"Them?" Her knee started to tremble for the tenth time that day.

"Yes. A double session. Nada and Rienne."

"Are you...naked?" she asked, hoping not to hear a certain answer.

"Emily! I'll see you tonight," he said sweetly, with what she thought was, but wasn't sure, a tone of humor.

She sat there stunned until Darren returned and stood in her doorway. She stood up. "Do you have the designs to leave with this guy for an estimate?" she asked quietly, staring at the wall.

"Done," Darren said, patting his tote bag.

"Then I'm ready. Let's go," she said as she walked toward him.

"Aren't you forgetting something?"

"Like what?"

"Like your purse and your phone."

"I didn't forget," Emily lied, "I was just about to get them."

TWENTY-SEVEN

THE CLOCK SAID eleven pm. He would be here any moment. Emily got out the eau de vie and two snifters. She opened the front door, leaving it ajar and then turned on the exterior light. She went to a corner of the front office, sat down on the sofa and waited for Chris, in the dark. She lit a lone candle and stared at the flickering shadows the candlelight cast on the walls, on the front door and, finally, on Chris as he softly wheeled his bike inside and leaned it against the entry wall. She studied him as he stood there. She no longer cared about Nada and Rienne.

The sex was getting rougher. No one seemed to mind. She would have to remember to clean off Kimiko's desk and look for her bra.

They had moved on to the bedroom for a tender version for round two. Afterwards, they cuddled closely and talked.

"What do you think about taking this to the next level," Chris said.

"You're still married. *Separated*. I thought you just wanted time apart from each other for a while."

"It's not going to work. I need more and you meet my needs. All of them," he said.

"Things are pretty good now between us, don't you think?"

"Yes. That's why I want more. Of you," he said.

"Then let's ease into it." As soon as she said those words, she regretted it because, in her head, Michael still owned her heart and maybe always would. "But tell me what the next level means, so I don't misunderstand you."

"We'll be exclusive to one another," he said.

"I'm ahead of you on that one," she said. She didn't want to say that she already thought they were exclusive to one another— one man at a time was enough for her to handle. She kissed him tenderly and then got up to run a bath.

He was washing her back, tracing her outline with the hand held spray when a phone rang. They let it go into voice mail. The phone beeped the urgent signal.

"It could be something with my kids," Chris said and went to check his phone, which was on the bedside table next to Emily's pet rescue application. "It's your phone. It says "Linda Sterling," he said as he walked back in the bathroom with Emily's cell.

"That's the third message she's left today, I better listen to it. Can you access it for me?"

He hit the voicemail button and followed the prompts. It was the same procedure on his phone, so he didn't have to ask. He hit the speakerphone button.

The messages rolled from the most recent: *"It's me, I'm at St. John's. I'm better, but I need you here. Hi, It's me. I'm at St. John's. Something happened. Call me or come by soon as you get this. Hi, It's me. I was attacked. I'll be okay, but everything hurts and I'm really scared. Call me at St. John's. I'll be here overnight at least. The cops are coming tomorrow morning."*

Emily and Chris looked at each other incredulously. "Wait, there's one more message," he said.

The final message was old, having been missed in the recent shuffle of confusion. It was from September 18th, about 12:30 am. It was a woman's voice, shrieking, and some kind of struggle going on: slapping, kicking, men swearing, things crashing and banging and then silence.

They looked at each other.

"What was that?" Chris asked. He thought that might have been the same night the cop had asked him about.

"I don't know. It sounds like a wrong number," Emily said, her heart racing. She knew exactly what it was. She changed the subject. "We have to go see Linda, right now."

"That was someone calling you for help," Chris said.

"Someone misdialed," Emily lied, sinking deeper into the bathtub.

"She was clearly in trouble," Chris said. "It was September 18th. Wasn't that also the night you were freaked out over something? Is that what was bugging you at the Hungry Cat?"

"I don't know anything about that call. It's the first time I've heard it," Emily said as she got out of the tub. Chris had a large towel ready for her. He wrapped her in it and dried her off with his strong hands.

"We'll go see Linda. Then you'll tell me about that phone call. We have to talk about it. I knew you were freaked out about something. If we are going to be closer, I need to know why you have been behaving strangely. Do know I told a detective I was with you that Sunday night the 17th from eight pm until the sun rose on the 18th."

He held her tightly, then stood back from her and looked into her eyes. This was the freaked-out Emily he was examining, but her remoteness made her even more enticing to him than the everyday Emily. They went for round three.

The sun was coming up. The perfect night had blended seamlessly into another perfect day.

"I have to take my kids to school. We can go see Linda after that," Chris said, as he brought her some coffee.

"I have to be at a jobsite then. It's okay; I'll go by myself. I'll call you after that," Emily said, sitting up in bed and wrapping her hands around the porcelain cup.

"I'm the pumpkin patch king this afternoon, so if I don't pick up, it's only because I'm up to my ears in jack-o-lanterns and hyper-active six year olds," he said, buttoning up his denim shirt.

She saw something in his eyes at that moment that told her no matter what, he just loved her. "I'll make some wall space for your bike rack," she said with a smile so achingly big, it felt like it belonged to someone else.

"And we'll pick out that rescue pup. Together," he said, as he took in how happy she now was.

TWENTY-EIGHT

THE WIDE RED WAY FINDING LINE on the floor went on and on. The abrupt click-click-click her four-inch high heels made on impact caused heads to look up from their tasks as she passed by. She stayed with the red line around corners, down long corridors, through several different nursing stations and departments, then continued through shorter corridors around several more corners and finally, the most straightforward of visual direction systems brought her to Linda's room. Well, she was pretty sure that's where she was. Emily took a closer look at the pile of puffiness, bruises and bandages that contained a person within. She bent down toward the face.

"Linda?"

"It's about fucking time." This came out of a mouthful of gauze.

"Jesus. I'm so sorry. I picked up my messages about three am. I had no idea. What happened?"

"It hurts to talk," Linda said slowly.

"Who did this to you?"

"Raiders fans," she said.

"Why?"

"My book research— didn't I tell you about it?"

"Yes, you did. At the Hungry Cat. My head was fucked up that night so I completely forgot about that. We left there fighting," Emily said.

"*You* were a first class asshole. I was trying to reason," Linda said.

"Oh crap. I owe you an apology. I'm sorry. I was out of control," Emily said.

"Thank you. Apology accepted. Anyway, I was doing so great with all the different teams; I collected over a hundred phone numbers. I can't believe how well it was going. I got a ton of material. Then, when I was wearing an Eagles cap— and I only wore it once— everything changed. It turns out I wore it in front of the wrong group of people. I don't recall too much after that."

"Someone beat you up for wearing an Eagles cap?"

"Not someone, a group of— make that a mob. They were wearing Raiders jerseys and those thuggy knit caps. I was tackled and the next thing I know, I wake up here."

"Thank God you're fine— or you will be fine. A new category for the book?"

"That's an idea. Maybe under the *"don't"* section." They broke into an easy laughter, as it hurt Linda to laugh much harder.

"A bit of advice. Stick to baseball," a rasp-tinged voice said from behind them. Baseball teams were next on her research list.

"We should talk then," Linda said to the stranger.

"Baseball's another story. We need to change the topic," another voice chimed in. Emily had her back to them. She thought she recognized the voices and was just about to place them.

"Linda Sterling? I'm Detective North. This is Detective De Meo. We'd like to show you photos of the men who we think did this to you," Detective North said as they walked into the room.

"And you are...? Why, Ms. Everheart, long time no see. Small world. Our paths cross again," De Meo said as he pulled up a chair next to the bed while staring past Linda, directly at Emily.

"You know each other?" Linda asked.

"We've met. Quite recently I might add," De Meo said. "How are you Ms. Everheart?" How are things at the office? Nice and quiet lately? What a coincidence that we see you here with another woman who's been a victim of an attack," De Meo said.

Linda didn't want to go there. Maybe the comment had something to do with Emily's behavior lately. She left it alone. Her friend would tell her when she was ready.

"I need to find the ladies room. I'll be right back," Emily said, ignoring De Meo. She found her way to the red line and then merged on to the yellow line to the restroom.

"Can you tell us if these are the men who did this to you?" Detective North said as he showed her some mug shots. Linda studied them closely.

"No, that's not them."

"Take another look," North said. Think about it. I know you've suffered some trauma."

"No, these aren't the guys," Linda said again, clearly in pain.

"Ms. Sterling, we have these guys in custody. They've assaulted, drugged and raped several women on the Westside in the past year. They also may be responsible for several missing women in the area. They live in the general vicinity where you were attacked," De Meo said.

"I understand. I don't want bad guys roaming the streets anymore than the next person. My vision may be blurred but these are not the guys."

"Ms. Sterling, these *are* the men who attacked you. They reside in the area. They have priors for attacking women. We have them. You just have to ID them," De Meo said as if she hadn't heard him the first time.

"Lay off, Joe," Detective North said. "Miss, we need you to be certain. That's all."

"I'll tell you how certain I am," Linda said as a colossal ache twisted through her skull and out her ears. "I *have* seen these guys around town. I don't know them. Have never talked to them. I can tell you that these are *not* the guys who attacked me."

"One more look. The report said it was dark when the attack took place. You're how old....? Perhaps your eyesight isn't as good as it use to be," De Meo said.

"Joe, I said leave it alone. Now Ms. Sterling, you said you've seen these guys around town. How recently? Where did you see them?" North asked.

"Didn't we see these guys one night?" Linda said to Emily just as she returned from the bathroom. Emily looked at the photos.

"I don't think so. No." Emily said as she scanned the photos of the Biscotti brothers.

"I think they were at Hal's that night," Linda said. "Judy was talking to them. I think. Do you remember?"

"That night is a blur to me— one too many Cosmos. I'm surprised you can remember anything," she said to Linda.

"Who's Judy?" Detective North asked Linda.

"Judy Cleveland, my literary agent. But what difference does it make? You said you already have these guys in jail."

Both North and De Meo became quiet. They both knew that name, but didn't know why. Emily thought that it was a good time for her to go. She was pretty sure she knew the reason for the detectives' silence.

"You'll excuse me," Emily said, "I have to get to a jobsite meeting." And without even saying goodbye to Linda, she made a bee-line for the wide red line and followed it all the way to the parking structure.

Traffic was terrible. It would take her longer than she had planned to get to the Gallery meeting. At a stop light, she called the office to let them know she may be late, and for Darren and Thomas to start without her.

Crossing the 405, it was stop and go, but mostly stop. She was thinking about looking into buying Candy's space. In her head, she owned the entire building and had the whole upper unit redesigned to suit her needs. She would turn the upstairs into a spacious home. The downstairs would be used solely for her business. But, then again, it was probably way too soon to talk to anyone about it.

It what seemed like an instant later, she was pulling up at the gallery. She barely remembered the drive. Somehow, she wasn't as late as she thought she would have been. Darren and Thomas hadn't even arrived yet. She turned to the back seat and rifled through a file folder. Emily pulled out Dar's purple tie that she had used to create the wall color. She stared at it, noticing that the tie was actually several different shades of other purples. I am insane, she thought, for using this color. Any other designer would have quit the project at the precise moment he took off his tie at that first meeting. But— money talks and, at the time, that was her mother tongue.

Once inside, she was awed at the pristine form of the gallery that was now taking. She had designed it that way, but until a design was built-out and realized, you never knew what, exactly, you would end up with. It was an emotional moment, as it always was at this stage, when all the elements fell into place as originally conceived. A huge sense of relief, mixed with satisfaction, reinforced in her the sense that she wasn't, as she had often feared, a fraud.

She did a double take as she saw Dar sporting an out-of-character casual linen blazer and trouser combo, walking across the main gallery.

"Frank," Dar, yelled to an unpopulated site. "Frank. Fra-ank. Frank. F R A N K!!!!"

"Yo! Here I am. Dar! Nice to see you" Frank yelled as he entered the space.

"Frank, it's really coming along. You're doing a great job. If I didn't see it with my own eyes, I wouldn't believe it," Dar said.

"Hey, thanks man. It was a weird plan to follow, but I was able to redesign it and solve all the problems to make it work. I can't tell you how many mistakes were in the drawings. Look at this reveal and the precision of it. And these grout joints over here are barely visible—"

"They're barely visible because I made you redo the half-inch joints you made because you didn't read the instructions for minimal grout joint thickness," Emily articulated very patiently but with varying levels of bitchiness.

"Dar, nice to see you, I didn't know you'd be here. I like your new look," Emily said.

"It's part of my new laid-back style. I have to get use to the idea that I look like I just got out of bed. A goatee is next," he said cheerfully as he stroked his chin. "I'm popping in today because I want to uncrate the art collection and start installing it. When can we do that?" Dar asked.

"In a few weeks. After we get the walls painted. In fact that's why I'm here today. None of the purple samples has been right," Emily said.

"You're just too frigging picky," Frank complained. "We made twenty-two samples and none of them are good enough for her. I have to pay the painter extra for that. His bid was for three color samples. Money, money, money, she sure likes to spend it." Frank said with mock exasperation, throwing up his arms and rolling his eyes.

"Let's take a look. I'd like to see the purples that aren't good enough," Dar said, quite bored. Frank walked them to the area where there were twenty-two, four-foot by four-foot purple samples on the wall. Each one was either identical or so close to identical to the next that the average person wouldn't be able to tell them apart.

"Frank," Emily said, getting back to proper business, "Where is the original blend that I gave you? It's not here."

"I didn't use it. This is a...better...quality paint. Make that more...*cost effective*," Frank said.

"You mean cheaper." Dar concluded. "How come I didn't see the cost savings on the last monthly budget comparison."

"Well, I haven't produced that paperwork yet," Frank mumbled.

Emily was about to accuse Frank of pocketing the difference, but just then Darren and Thomas showed up with the original color mix.

In a choreographed sequence that kept a metronomic rhythm, Darren dug a paintbrush out of his bag while Thomas sanded down a six inch by six-inch spot on the wall. Darren dusted off the area and Thomas carefully applied the proper purple paint on the wall. Then Darren got out a blow dryer and ran it over the new sample. Emily pulled out the tie in question from her bag and had Thomas stand there holding it next to the six by six proper purple paint sample. Darren then held up a bizarre looking device and illuminated the fresh sample under various forms of lighting temperatures: natural daylight, incandescent, fluorescent, and LED. Emily crossed her arms. "That's our color," she said triumphantly.

"Hey, that's my tie! I've been looking for it," Dar said, without commenting on the proper purple paint.

"It's what we based the color on at the first meeting," Emily said, being careful not to imply anything about Dar's state of memory.

"What a great idea. Using my tie! You know me so well," Dar said as he left, without saying goodbye, but with a very big smile on his face.

"I thought you said the tie color was his idea," Thomas said.

"It doesn't matter anymore. We have another satisfied client," Emily said to the boys.

"You win," Frank said as Darren handed him the proper purple paint pot. "But, hey, you know, I was a color specialist."

"We know. You played one on TV," Darren said.

TWENTY-NINE

I T TOOK NORTH AND DE MEO a while to clear the lobby reception desk at the Big Agency where Judy Cleveland had her office, and it wasn't because of security. The battery of young receptionists, male and female, was engaged in non-stop phone answering and order-taking from unseen outsiders and interoffice staff.

Finally, one young male cast a quick glance to North and asked in rapid-fire speech, as he turned back to the switchboard, "Who-are-you-here-to-see-what-time-is-your-appointment?"

North couldn't understand a word the receptionist had said so he showed him his badge. By this time the young man was onto another phone call and task and didn't look up. After several seconds, North realized he missed his moment and wasn't going to get it back unless he made himself known some other way. North dropped his badge on the young man's keyboard. The young man picked up the badge, glanced at it and handed it back to North while continuing to deal with the non-stop phone calls.

"Take a seat over there and we'll call you in a few minutes," the receptionist said in the same zippy cadence, without taking his eyes off his monitor.

North and De Meo sat on a sleek, but incredibly uncomfortable, architecturally designed sofa placed at an improper viewing angle to a huge contemporary mural by some famous dead modern artist. They waited. And waited. The pace at the reception desk did not abate. After a half-hour, De Meo got up and went to the young man who had directed them to sit.

"We've been waiting for thirty minutes. We'd like to see Judy Cleveland. Now. Even a gay-boy receptionist like you should be able to handle a girlie job like that. It's not like you went to Harvard—"

"Princeton," the young man said, cutting off De Meo, without looking up. "But I don't expect someone like you to know the difference. Ms. Cleveland has been in a meeting all day. It looks like she had a break two minutes ago, if you go with this man who is walking up behind you right now, he'll escort you to Ms. Cleveland's office. Please don't fret, he can find his way because *he* graduated from Harvard." De Meo stood there, speechless for once. Brett Hyatt, the young man still juggling a cell phone in each ear, put out his hand to greet the guests as they turned to face him. Both cops looked Brett up and down, fixing their gaze on his expensive, ultra-low cut loafers, before they each shook his hand.

They arrived at Judy Cleveland's spacious, but wrongly adorned, office. Judy was standing at her desk going through a pile of manuscripts. Brett gestured for North and De Meo to enter, closed the door and showed the men to a sofa that was completely covered in dog hair. Brett went over to a cabinet and opened it. He removed two bottles of water, two cocktail napkins and two glass tumblers that were etched with JCA, placed them on an antique silver serving tray and brought them over to the two men. Neither North, nor De Meo, used a glass or a napkin.

"We have here Officers De Meo and North," Brett said to Judy.

"Detectives," North and De Meo said at the same time.

"Whatever. Gentlemen, you have five minutes," Judy said without looking up from her search. Her hunched-over posture barely changed as she hovered over her desk.

A couple of mug shots of the Biscotti brothers landed right under her nose. She looked up at North and De Meo, insulted and appalled, with her mouth open, but devoid of words.

"You said five minutes. So I'm being time efficient," North said. He knew how to get people's attention by giving them their own attitude— it always worked. They could never handle their own attitudes being perpetrated upon themselves.

"What do you want?" Judy queried. This pair disgusted her, with their rumpled coats and off-putting style.

"We are hoping you can help us. Can you identify these men? Look closely," North said.

Judy studied him skeptically. She put on her reading glasses on for a closer look at the photos.

"No," she said after perfunctory glance. "Why would I know these people?"

"Look again," De Meo said.

"No, I don't know them. Is that it? I have another meeting in—"

"You've been seen talking to them," De Meo said, cutting her and her meeting off.

"I talk to a lot of people. Doesn't mean I know them," Judy said.

"So, you've talked to them?" De Meo said.

"No, I've never talked to them. Is that it?"

"When was the last time you saw Candy Jones?"

"I don't know that person," Judy said.

"Do you know Emily Everheart?"

"No."

"She's a friend of a client of yours, Linda Sterling. You do know who Linda Sterling is, right?" De Meo said.

"Yes, I know Linda," Judy said.

"You rejected a cooking manuscript from Candy Jones. With a letter, that you personally signed," De Meo said.

"I don't write them or sign them. The signature is a stamp. We send out— how many of those Brett?— each week," Judy asked, clueless.

"A hundred, maybe." Brett said while multi-tasking across from Judy at her desk. He caught a glimpse of the mug shots, while reaching to answer Judy's phone.

"What *is* this all about?" Judy asked again of North and De Meo as they got up.

"Candy Jones is missing. Linda Sterling was attacked and savagely beaten. You are the link between them. Call us if you remember anything about these men. We're holding them in custody, but we need to connect some dots to slam dunk our case," said North.

"By the way, like you care, but Sterling was repeatedly punched and kicked in her face and head. But she'll be okay. She's lucky she's not brain damaged from it," De Meo said.

"She needs to put the finishing touches on her book, so yes, I care," Judy said.

"You care about her book. People like you don't care about other people," De Meo said.

"So what. I love writing and I hate writers. And I don't have to reason with you lowbrow cock-suckers. Out. Now," she said waiving her hand as if to brush them away.

"Gentlemen, I'll see you out," Brett said professionally.

"That's okay, we'll find our way," North said as they walked out of Judy's office and started down a massive corridor of endless, sleek cubicles and full-height glass paneled offices.

"This way," North said to De Meo, as they walked through a pair of doors, onto a catwalk over the atrium, through another pair of automatic doors and into a unisex employee lounge furnished with floor-to-ceiling mirrors, chrome framed German-designed daybeds and waterless urinals.

Brett cleared the water bottles and prepped the area for the next meeting. In doing so, he picked up something on the sofa and examined it. It was a roach clip and with a roach attached.

"You know, those twins were at Hal's. You spent a long time talking to them. They were pitching their book idea and they gave you their business card, which you gave to Linda Sterling, who introduced you to her friend Emily that night," he said.

"How can you remember such an inconsequential series of shit," Judy barked.

"Might I remind you, you pay me big bucks for all kinds of things, including observing and remembering details. That's not part of your everyday skill set."

"I'm totally lost. So what do I do now? Am I supposed to call and tell them that you remembered this?"

"No, not at all," Brett said with a very serious look as he took a seat and crossed his legs, revealing tanned ankles.

"You can't tell me this shit and then expect me to forget about it. Telling them could be the right thing to do," Judy said.

"It's not the right thing to do," Brett assured her.

"Because?"

"Well, there isn't anything in it to benefit us. Those yutzes already have the brutes in custody. Don't waste another second on it.

"Furthermore, you never read that cooking manuscript. The readers were passing the manuscript around because it had food smears throughout, and the margin notations were a scream! And who sends a hard copy of a manuscript anymore? Anyone, even a brain-dead knows to send a PDF file. And it's only because of the state of the book that I read the coverage. It was just awful. Remember what you always tell me? *At the Judy Cleveland agency, we don't do awful.*"

THIRTY

JUAN, THE NEW UPHOLSTORER, was holding his breath. He had been working on fabricating this unique mock-up for a several days now. His new designer client was inspecting the one-of-a-kind adjustable dining chair. She was testing it out by straddling it in various positions that all looked sexual. This made Juan quite uncomfortable. Finally she was done.

"These are the most comfortable chairs I have ever sat in," Emily said with a satisfied look.

"The way you were using it, I was thinking I should have made you a bed," Juan said.

"A sneaky sensuality. Oh yes," Emily said dreamily.

"It's pretty obvious, Mrs. Everheart," Juan said.

"Call me Emily," she said. She hadn't been Mrs. Everheart for a long time. "These chairs have just the right amount of mystery—they are beautiful. I'll sign off on the order now so you can make them all."

"It's a complicated design. Very intricate. It was so much more time than I thought even though I looked over your drawings well. More time than I can eat. I'm sorry, but I can't honor the original quote that I gave you when you and Darren were here before," Juan said.

Emily's body language said *oh no*!

"How much more do you think it will cost?" she asked.

"Another two-fifty per chair," Juan said sadly.

"How about if we use a less costly wood?" Emily asked.

"Ms. Emily, it's the labor. These details take so much time. It will be the same amount of time with each one."

"What kind of detail can you give me for the price you quoted?"

"I recommend we lose the fully reclining position and the solid bronze detail. You could do a faux finish to look like bronze."

"Ugh. Let me think about it. I'll call you tomorrow. Thanks for staying open late for me," Emily said as she brushed some workroom debris off her sweater and left.

It was dark when she got back to the office. Everyone had already gone home. Emily kicked off her shoes and left them on the floor in the entry. She walked into her office and was about to check on how much they had left in the Dufrene budget to offset the additional chair fabrication cost, when she noticed a check taped to her monitor. On it, stamped in red, was *Account Closed*. Just above the stamp was the account name: *Vivian Wyntor*. The check was for money owed and for future expenditures, most of which Emily had placed deposits on. Emily immediately called Vivian Wyntor. The phone was disconnected. She tried the cell. No answer. She tried Ralph. Certainly he would pick up. His outgoing message said he was on an extended holiday abroad and wasn't taking calls. Emily screamed, grabbed her hair at her forehead and pulled hard. She would have to go to the Wyntor residence first thing tomorrow, just before the Think Tank presentation.

She retraced her relationship with Viv to see if she had missed something. There had been no red flags. The conversations had always been clear. No passive/aggressive behavior. And the woman was flush with old money. It was simply inexplicable to Emily. There was nothing she could do until tomorrow.

She needed to relax, fast. She reached under her desk and took a great cab from a case she had just received from a grateful vendor. She went into the kitchen and placed it in the freezer to cool it down a bit. It was an old trick Michael had taught her. Too bad Chris was busy this evening with his kids. She had to get her mind off of Viv Wyntor for the evening. She focused her thoughts on the upstairs layout if she took over the space. She had several ideas, but needed to get them down on paper to flush out details and, ultimately, costs. First though, she'd make herself eat something, so she'd have a full tummy when she got plowed shortly. She assembled a plate of leftovers and reheated them in the speed oven. She turned on the fifteen-inch plasma, moved it to the table and went to get the wine. She peeled back the foil cap and carefully inserted the corkscrew while standing in front of the open fridge. She could hear the television in the background.

Breaking news was the headline. Every news story these days was renamed *breaking news,* she thought. A young DA was holding a press conference. Flanked by a crush of cameras, the young DA was talking about going forward with her case against the Biscotti brothers, and citing all the charges she had filed against them. Emily walked away from the fridge, bottle in hand, leaving the door ajar, and stared at the television. Photos of several women, including a glamour shot of Candy, were scrolling across the screen. Not only had she never seen a glamorous Candy, there was something about the young DA that captured her attention. She couldn't place her, but was pretty sure she knew her from somewhere. Finally, the DA's name popped onto the screen: *Holden Knox-Everheart.*

Everheart?

No, it can't be, she thought. It was hard to make out what was being said at the press conference with the mob of reporters shouting questions. It was quite a chaotic scene.

Then the television camera was jostled so that the angle was just out of the DA's frame. In the adjacent crowd there was someone Emily was *certain* she knew. Someone who owned her heart.

Michael Everheart.

She gasped. This was the same woman Emily had seen at the rug showroom. The same woman with the awful taste in rugs, acting like she owned the place. The DA The Waxer had mentioned. The same DA whose fiancé sent her in for a smoothie. She screamed NO at the top of her lungs until she passed out.

Candy wouldn't stop laughing at Emily. Belly laughing, maniacally. Big gaping mouth, dirty cigarette breathe. Hardy-fucking-har. Har, har, har. Loud, grating laughter accompanied by snorts and screeching howls. Har, har, har, snort. Laughing like that, at Emily. Emily was voiceless when she screamed back at Candy. Emily swung over and over at Candy and kept missing. Candy kept laughing at Emily, harder and harder. There was no end in sight. Emily covered her ears, but that didn't help. The noise was inside her brain. It was now so loud that—

Emily came to just then. Cape Fear was on TV. It wasn't Candy laughing at her now, it was Robert De Niro, seated in a theatre, laughing insanely and scaring Nick Nolte, Jessica Lange and Juliette Lewis out of their pants. It took a moment, but as her consciousness increased, Emily realized it had just been a horrible and agonizing dream. Max Cady wasn't tormenting her. Candy *was* tormenting her. Holden Knox-Everheart *was* tormenting her. And Vivian Wyntor *was* tormenting her. Emily cringed in empty anguish. All she had wanted to do, she recalled, was to open a bottle of wine, eat and zone out.

Emily lay on the polished concrete floor. Her head hurt. She winced as she felt the stinging bump above her brow. She was covered in blood. At a second glance, she realized it was the expensive cab as she recognized the earthy bouquet. Apparently, when she went down earlier, she brought the Opus One with her. She knew the acid in the wine would leave a discoloration on the floor, but didn't care about that right now.

THIRTY-ONE

DARREN PULLED UP in front of Vivian Wyntor's stately, but modern-chic, residence. Emily opened the door before he came to a full stop. She tried to get out, but her seat belt was still fastened. She knew they only had forty-five minutes to deal with this before the Think Tank presentation. Thomas pulled up behind them in his Escalade. She had him follow in case they needed to remove anything from the house to recoup any impending losses.

"I can go in with you, if you'd like," Darren said to her.

"That's a good idea," Emily said. "You can keep me from killing her." Darren motioned to Thomas to join them. They walked passed the pair of art deco onyx panthers and up the white terrazzo floating steps, over the architectural Koi pond and stood under the cantilevering flat portico. Emily stood in the precise spot that would automatically ring the door chime. They waited. After a minute, she jumped on the spot to ring the chime again. She also knocked on the eleven-foot high solid mahogany front door. And knocked. No answer. Big surprise, she thought. She knew she was fucked.

"I don't know what to do," Emily said. "We can't even get in for a repo."

"It won't come to that," Darren said.

"We have to face the fact that it could," Emily said. She rubbed her eyes and forehead, massaging her bump. "No sense standing around here. We've got to get to the presentation—"

"What on earth are you doing here?" Viv Wyntor asked, naked and holding Mr. T as the front door was automatically pivoting open. Viv was clearly indignant. Darren and Thomas lowered their eyes. Mr. T growled.

"Viv, I'm concerned. I tried to call you. Your check was returned from the bank saying the account—" Emily said.

"Yes, I know. My assets are frozen. My accounts are closed. I have no control over this. The Feds are investigating my ex and his family. It's not the first time. In my opinion, it's all a wild goose chase. Anyway, I can't talk about it. It depresses me," Viv Wyntor said. Naked.

"Vivian, we are in the middle of huge expenditures. Whom can we talk to about this, if not you?" Emily asked.

"Normally, I'd say my lawyer or someone at his firm. But they're being investigated too," Viv Wyntor said. "Help nowadays, you can't trust them."

And thirty minutes later, with the Escalade being weighed down by three huge rugs, they pulled up to the Water Garden Complex— one of the hottest business addresses in Santa Monica. They plucked rug schmutz off themselves and Emily touched up the make up on her forehead. The concealer that covered her bruise had sweated off during the rug recoup.

Emily, Darren and Thomas stood back when they finished going over everything. Exhausted but thrilled, they knew the presentation won over the Clients. They were receptive to every detail and paid close attention to the minutia as well as the big events of the plan, and no rude interruptions— unlike most clients. Emily and her guys beamed at the group of Thinkers, waiting for the usual questions to be asked. The Thinkers smiled back, politely. No questions to be asked, so Emily took the meeting to the next step.

"I have prepared this contract which allows us to proceed with the build-out, once you approve our presentation. So, if you'll just sign here," Emily said, with her winning smile and professional diction as she flipped to the signature page and handed it to the lead scientist.

"I thought we were getting French country. Like Pierre Deux," the thirty-nine year old scientist, Dr. Miller said.

"I don't know why, but I had pictured petite stripes and floral patterns, too," another Thinker, Dr. Bhipkin said.

"There's no blue. I love blue. On the TV shows, they say it keeps us calm," the last of the trio, Dr. Schmitt said.

"If I may," an unknown, proper looking, mature woman interjected. She had entered the room during the last five minutes of the fifty-minute presentation.

"Have we met?" Emily asked on the verge of erupting.

"I'm Dr. Miller's mother, Mrs. Miller. I've decorated for him his whole life. I insisted on sitting in and offering my opinion."

Emily girded herself. No other kind of hack-non-pro presented adversity more than a Mother-ecorator.

"First of all, this is all wrong! I can't believe you call yourself an Interior Designer! Why I could do better with my eyes closed. I told my son you cherry-picked your references and not to hire you. And now you've wasted so much time on this. How much are you charging my son for this silly design circus?"

Emily had already been worn down by the morning's events and now, this. The dreadful mother-monster sapped the last bit of energy Emily had. She couldn't even manage another word. All she could muster was eye contact with Darren. He understood. He would have to take over right now.

Darren grabbed the contract and scanned it. "Why, Mrs. Miller," he said charmingly, "I don't see your name on the contract. Let's see here, we have Dr. Miller, Dr. Bhipin and Dr. Schmitt— no Mrs. Miller. We would have taken your thoughts into consideration if it had been explained to us that you were to be a part of the design committee. No problem, we will draft a new contract and start—"

"Contract, schmontract! I'll do the decorating myself!" the horrid old gal bellowed.

"Doctors, please, if you want design *à la Provence,* we can do that. It's not a problem," Darren said emphatically. Then Emily's torso started to quiver, then convulse, and within ten seconds, she threw up all over the drone-inspired 3-D model.

"If that's not a deal breaker, I don't know what is," Thomas whispered to Darren.

THIRTY-TWO

BACK AT THE OFFICE that afternoon, Emily washed her face for the third time since they returned— her sweating had turned to a downpour. She sent Kimiko, Cookie and Toshi home early because she couldn't handle talking to anyone right now, or even seeing anyone. She told Darren and Thomas to bring the rugs back to Joe and to see if she could get a full refund. This was the time when she really valued her supplier relationships. When they would help her get out of a hellhole by just saying, *Okay, whatever you want.*

She was hopeful she could resurrect the Think Tank project. The nagging question was, did she want to subject herself to a prosaic design when she knew the design they presented had been kick-ass perfect. Not to mention, oh yeah, that functional thing.

Looking for something to take her mind off of both Viv Wyntor and the Think Tank, Emily went through the mail. It was mostly junk, but the new Architectural Digest was there, wrapped in it's pristine, clear plastic. There was, as usual, a magnificent home on the cover, which caught her eye. She didn't feel like reading at that moment, so she tossed it on top of the eighteen inch high stack of shelters-to-be-read on her credenza, next to a backlog of blank crossword puzzles.

She then checked the calendar. They were scheduled to be at the Dufrene's tomorrow morning with Bob the engineer to do a run-through of the floor lift. Emily was looking forward to seeing the floor in action. The impending success of the design would place her firm at an entirely new level. At least, she thought, there was something positive on the horizon.

She realized Thanksgiving was creeping up fast— which made her groan. She equated holidays more with project deadlines than with family, friends or religion. This added to her stress level because she had two projects coming to fruition: The Gallery and the Dufrene's flying dining room. But, Thanksgiving could be handled. Christmas/Channukah was bad, but Passover/Easter was worse. First one group of subs takes their holiday, then the other denomination takes theirs, thus making for one really long holiday season with lots of work-time lost. Not to mention, that it seemed like subs' wives were always having babies at the most inconvenient times. She made a note to herself about finding trades people that didn't worship anything but work itself.

Personally, there was some good news. Linda Sterling had recovered beautifully and was having a bash at Froggie's in Topanga Canyon tomorrow night to celebrate not only the release of dueling books and her birthday, but also to announce some huge news. It would be a welcome distraction for Emily. She was really looking forward to it. Chris wanted to join her, but wasn't sure if he could schedule it in between all the kids' activities.

Emily then perused some questions and comments Kimiko and Cookie had left regarding their e-design projects. They were concerned they were taking too much time to complete the e-work and wanted to consult with Emily before they continued on. They both had detailed their time logged to date against the fees that Emily was charging for the service. Even at a glance, Emily could tell the time they were spending more than tipped the scales in favor of the client. In short, the e-staff had been working too many hours to justify the flat fee idea.

As she read the task description for each hour, she could tell they were working quite efficiently. She did not see any wasted or duplicate effort in any of the descriptions. While e-design was all the rage right now with the younger clients, it was nothing but a big money loser for Emily Everheart Interior Design. If she wanted to be competitive in the e-business, she'd have to dumb down the process drastically. Maybe, she thought, she'd have them randomly download tear sheets, put them in a pile and pull ideas from a given amount of furnishings and colors. No more individual design. It would be egalitarian. Maybe she'd have the girls pull together three different designs, and just sell those as is. Let the consumer select one of the options. It was good enough for Henry Ford. But, what if they wanted to substitute a piece from another option? Would Emily allow that? The stress of having to re-think this unprofitable service gave her a whopper of a headache that morphed into another raging hot flash.

This was fuck-all. Her life, fuck all. Had it been a big mistake to let Michael go? Loser, loser, loser. She set the work notes aside, googled Holden Knox, clicked in to an unprotected Facebook page and stalked her replacement. She clicked on the Mexican honeymoon photo album, recognized in the blurry frozen frame shot her Ex's body (the extended play version). She didn't want to, but she did anyway, click on the still and watch the video animate.

He is so beautiful, she thought.

And, an impressively pliable and steamy Holden, who had recently purchased and installed a super-sized set of melons, was perpetually running her tongue over her lips while looking into the camera she was holding. Holden let go of the camera as she ascended; howling like a she-wolf, into the ethereal world of orgasm, then groped for the device once the perfect sensation arced. This time the background came into view— an open bottle of *Cialis* on a gaudy bedside table that matched a tacky over-scaled carved headboard in the shape of a bunch of huge bananas. Holden tumbled on to a jumble of flabby throw pillows and zoomed in on Michael as he entered her and loved her precisely. Emily watched the fuck-fest with a pit in her gut as Michael flipped Holden on to her belly, camera still rolling from over her moist shoulder, aimed exactingly at his seed as it spurted seemingly endless all over Holden's juicy ass as the lovebirds nestled amongst the mishmash of tasteless pillows.

I must stop loving him. I must. Right now.

The phone rang. It was late for most business calls, but she wearily answered. The connection was bad. Someone, a man, was asking for Candy. Emily's jaw tightened.

She clicked out of Holden Knox's Facebook page.

"There's no one here named Candy," Emily said as she realized she had just clicked the friend request by mistake.

"I said, I'm looking for Edward," the voice said, the connection now clear.

"There's no Candy here, I told you," Emily snapped, and hung up on the caller. She stared at the computer, the friend request window still on the screen. Crap.

She turned off the lights and headed to bed before anything else bad could happen. She had to put the day to an end. She had every intention of sleeping through the next ten hours. Tomorrow morning everything would be fine. It would be a brand new day with brand new energy. She would have a brand new attitude. The woes of today would not even enter her mind.

THIRTY-THREE

THE NEXT MORNING, Emily directed Cookie and Kimiko to dream up some scaled down options for e-decorating via a terse questionnaire. She told Toshi to add shopping carts to the website so consumers could pay for e-services and design phone consultations via Pay Pal prior to services being rendered. It was beneath her usual work ethic, but the design world was devolving rapidly and she was confident that these changes would help her exploit this recent phenomenon and keep her business on track.

Both Kimiko and Cookie thought they could make it work— even though neither had worked in such a dumbing-down of the thought-process. Designers are trained for years to find solutions in an unhurried, rational yet artistic manner. Emily had to retrain the young designers to provide loglines instead of novels.

It was a little after nine a.m. Emily grabbed her bag and walked outside. Thomas and Darren would be pulling up in a few moments to pick her up to go over to the Dufrene remodel. Emily took a moment to study the loft from the exterior. She had come up with a design for the façade, and was now visualizing her idea. The early sunlight had a bright pink tone to it— a result of the nearby raging wild fires. Tiny flecks of ash were floating in the air. The bright light quality gave the loft an imaginary and welcoming appearance. Emily examined the roofline, the gutters and the fenestrations. She could restore the industrial-style large windows.

The door would have to be replaced, as it was borderline inoperable, not to mention unsightly. She looked towards Candy's door. Something was different. She noticed the crime scene tape was gone. She had gotten used to it being there. With an unsettled feeling, she wondered what the absence of the bright yellow band meant.

The entire labor crew was there, on stand-by, in case any moving part of the floor had to be tweaked. When Emily entered the site, they applauded her and her team. Emily, touched by the gesture, fought back tears.

"We're just making our client's wish come true, nothing more. That's why we're all in this business! I couldn't have done it without Thomas and Darren. Nor could we have made it a reality without Bob, the best engineer in the world, and you guys, the star crew of America. You worked your asses off," she said. "And, the best news is, the Dufrenes will have a flying dining room for their Thanksgiving dinner party next week!" More applause, hugs and cheers of support. Everyone high-fived and congratulated one another. Emily was so relieved; she couldn't hold back the tears of joy.

"I have to say you were right again, Emily. We tested it three times and it works better than I imagined it would. Plus, it's so quiet. I am just tickled with it. You know, I started in this business a long time ago with a pencil and a slide rule," Bob the engineer said, shaking his head. Then he turned to his crew and said, "Okay, fellows, take your places. Let's show our star designer here that she can design anything and we can build anything." Bob walked over to the *Homeworks* wall screen. Emily took a deep breath. Thomas put his arm around her. With her other hand she grabbed Darren and pulled him into the huddle. They giggled nervously in anticipation.

"Ready, everyone? One, two, three," Bob said. Then he touched the prompt on the control pad. The floor started to retract and the table plateau started to rise. "Oh my," said Emily. She was in heaven.

Once the dust cloud settled and the noise abated, Bob the engineer yelled for a head count. The crew was all accounted for, as were Darren and Thomas. Emily emerged from under the crumpled and crashed flying dining room covered in debris. She began removing dust from her nostrils and ears and said to Bob tearfully, "We really have to fix this by Thanksgiving."

THIRTY-FOUR

LATER THAT DAY, Emily texted Linda Sterling saying that she didn't feel up to coming to the bash tonight. She was living through the mother of all bad weeks and she didn't want to have to talk about all the shit that was storming down on her head at the moment. She blamed her not wanting to go out on the close by hot and hungry wildfires that had the city on edge.

Linda texted back: *Chill. You and I are fireproof.*

Emily laughed at that. It felt good. It reminded her of what the evening could be like. She relented and responded: *Let's hope the hell so.*

Hating herself at the moment and wanting to pretend she was someone else, Emily dressed up. No one ever dressed up— one dressed down— for a Topanga joint. She decided on a glamour-hip combo of low rise, boot cut, tight jeans with a long, v-necked ultra-sheer blouse with the appropriate bra and an attention getting choker. She did her hair on the full side, wearing it down, but swept it to the side so her right eye was half covered. She put on more make up than usual, accenting her eyes and her lips. She slipped on a pair of low-heeled, strappy sandals, then decided they were way too sensible and went for something more carefree— a pair of over-sexed towering high-heels in a metal-studded black leather.

En route to Topanga Canyon, Emily pulled into the Von's on Sunset and Pacific Coast Highway to pick up a birthday card for

Linda. She selected a card that said how great Linda looked for her age. To top it off the card had noise in it— the late Rick James singing, *"She's a superfreak, she's super freaky..."* when opened.

There was only one woman in front of Emily in the check-out line but she was taking FOREVER to find her money. Emily waited patiently and glanced at the magazine rack. Architectural Digest was front and center— the same issue she had just received and tossed in her to-be-read stack. This was, however, the news-stand version, where they put the celebrity portrait on the cover instead of a house. But this was not just a celebrity on the cover. It was Reese Witherspoon *and Editha Eggers.* Emily picked up the issue and read the cover: *Reese and Editha: A Dazzling Duo collaborate on a Dreamy Santa Barbara Villa.*

Emily urgently flipped through the magazine and scanned the editorial, then back to the cover portrait: Ms. Witherspoon in a sporty vest and horsey boots along with Editha Eggers in an über couture Lacroix gown, triumph glowing from their éclat smiles. The hot-shit duet were lolling on the cool, rolling lush lawn of the latest Witherspoon estate, and toasting each other with grace-ful Baccarat flutes filled with pink champagne. Stylish purebred horses grazed in the pastoral distance. "Oh crap," Emily said to no one in particular.

"Next!" the cashier hollered at her. Emily shoved the maga-zine back on the stand— bending the cover in doing so, and paid for the birthday card with exact change to make for a quicker get-away. She stormed out of the supermarket and ran for her car. She stumbled in the parking lot (those stupid-ass heels) and hit the asphalt, tearing her jeans at the knee and landing flat on her face. She wanted to lay there, face down, and just die. A panhan-dler walked over and picked her up. "Yo, Natalie Wood," he said, "slow down!" It had been at least twenty years since she had been likened to the late screen goddess, but it didn't matter to her at the moment.

Prickly thoughts prowled through Emily's mind as shift-ing weaves of dusk light lurked across her face as she zigzagged through Topanga's chasms and gullies. She didn't care about her jeans; the ripped knee could easily pass for fashion sense. She pounded the dashboard and fought back tears that would ruin her make-up. Apt lyrics came from the radio: *"I been around in Donkeytown too long, baby too long. Checking out of Donkeytown. So long, so long, so long."*

She made the left into Froggie's driveway and went down the slope, past the Institute of Courage— whatever that was— and squeezed in between a Prius and a vintage pick-up truck in the already packed lot. Echoing voices and music boomed down to the woodsy parking area. The large windows above glowed like lanterns. She grabbed the birthday card out of her bag, wrote something pithy, signed it and stuffed it back in the envelope. She got out of the car and navigated the uneven, meandering steps that led to Froggie's back entrance. Linda had booked the cavernous dining room. It was already rollicking.

"Emily's here," Linda yelled. Everyone, quite happy already, cheered. Emily went over and hugged Linda. "You look great! Chris is supposed to be here any minute. He wants to surprise you," Linda said. "Don't tell him I told you."

"Fabulous! Yes, yes, yes," Emily said. Seeing him would put her in a better mood— exactly what she needed. This would be their first official get-together out of bed.

A young surfer-cum-server came by with a tray of the signature party drink in mason jars: Froggie's version of a Margarita. Linda grabbed one and gave it to Emily. Emily raised it up to Linda's drink.

"Happy birthday, my friend. So what's the big news you're going to tell us all?" Emily asked.

"I'm waiting until Chris and a few others are here before I blab. Say hi to Judy Cleveland, my agent," Linda said as Judy and Brett squeezed through.

"Why would I do that?" Emily said sarcastically, as Judy and Brett walked right by without so much as a glance. "But, what I *will* do is go sit by that beautiful, roaring fire and wait for Chris,"

Emily said as she zipped over to the cozy nook next to the fire-place. She couldn't believe the nook was empty; it was the best seat in the room by far. The fact that the fire was going was a little cheeky, she thought, considering the uncontainable wildfires burning at the edges of L.A.

She finished her drink and grabbed a second from the serving surfer. He also brought her some guac and chips. He gave her a sly smile, and more than once. She laughed to herself. Yeah, right, she thought. It had to be the choker.

She saw Chris come through the front entrance. He looked stressed. She wasn't use to seeing him that way. He was snapping at someone, but she couldn't tell who it was; she didn't see another person with him. Then she noticed Chris was looking downward. The crowd opened up and then she saw who Chris was snapping at— his little son, who was having a world-class tantrum. He was also dragging his daughter by the hand, who clearly did not want to be in this place. And, he had the pre-tot on his back. Emily couldn't believe her eyes. Well, maybe that's what he meant by taking our relationship to the next level, she thought. She chugged the rest of her drink, sure that she would need it. There goes the rest of my night, she thought cynically. Maybe the surfer would have to do.

She saw Chris hug Linda. She then saw Linda direct him to where Emily was. He looked over to the fireplace and saw Emily standing there staring at him. Emily managed to raise her hand in a wave. Chris and his kids made their way over to the fireplace.

"Kids," he said, "this is my friend, Emily."

The kids stared at Emily suspiciously. "Pleased to meet you," Emily said.

"This is Daniel. He's six. And this is Leah, she's four," Chris said. The kids grabbed on to Chris and hugged him snuggly, pressing their little faces into his legs so they didn't have to look at this Emily lady in this weird place with all these odd-looking grown-ups.

Daniel turned his head toward Emily and said, "I can see your underwear," and turned back into hiding.

"She's wearing Marshmallow's collar! And her pants are ripped," Leah cried out and then hid her face again.

"Oh dear!" Emily said, as she placed her hand on her choker.

"Underwear and rips are good things," Chris said. Then he looked into Emily's eyes with that look he had. "And doggie collars are really good." She got the message and relaxed.

"So I passed the friend test. I'm approved now?" Emily asked.

Just then the pre-tot spit up on Chris. He had a burp cloth handy and dabbed it up. No big thing. "This is Megan," he said as he gestured over his shoulder to the dyspeptic jellybean.

The guests were all milling toward the front of the dining room, near the fireplace where Emily and Chris were. Brett Hyatt stood up in front of everyone and lifted his mason jar margarita.

"Linda Sterling, I don't see you," Brett said with his hand over his eyes shielding the light. "Get your tukhus up here."

Linda made her way through the crowd. She was beaming and waving to everyone. Brett continued his speech, "We have some great news to share with all of Linda's closest friends and associates. We, Judy and I, are happy to say that not only are both of Linda's aftermarket dating books being released simultaneously, and bound for number one— and two— we have also closed a ground-breaking deal for Linda Sterling to be, THE Pro-dating expert on a major network show— "lots of cheers and whoops and hollers interrupted the speech— "and, THE anti-dating expert on a competing, major network show!"

The room went silent. "What did you say, I didn't hear you right," someone yelled.

Linda grabbed center stage. "You all heard right— and yes, it is completely absurd, but who cares! Judy closed an unprecedented deal— that's why she's RICH! I will be THE expert on dating on two competing networks. An anti-dating expert because of my first book, and a pro-dating expert because of my second book."

Everyone looked over to Judy Cleveland. She stood up and said, "Don't even ask and I'm not taking any new clients right now, so keep your pitches and scripts to yourselves." Everyone shouted their approvals and the alcohol continued to flow freely.

"Cake for everybody, right now," Linda yelled and directed everyone to the dessert table. The serving surfer was slicing a beautiful cake. Emily, Chris and the kids headed over to get some.

"What a pretty cake," young Leah said, excited.

"Thanks. We had to make it in-house," the surfer said, "I heard our usual pastry chef was murdered."

"What does murder mean?" four-year-old Leah asked Emily.

The view into the party room from the hall hid nothing and no one. "Our entire cast of characters is here tonight," De Meo said as he observed the gathering. He looked behind him to where he thought North was. The men's room door opened. North and his trademark swelling mass of cannabis smoke walked over to De Meo as he tough-guy-snuffed-out the fiery end of a blunt with his fingers.

THIRTY-FIVE

THE GREY RUBBER CLOGS quietly swooshed as they moved along on top of the red paint remnants that once constituted a line. The clogs moved confidently and with an air of perky joy. They made a detour at a dark, unoccupied nursing station to pick up a yellow legal pad, an alphabet chart and a pen. The youthful gait slowed and exchanged greetings with some blood-stained rubber clogs and then continued at a easy pace off the main line and into a large patient recovery room with several beds, only one of which was occupied. The aide flipped the light switch and waited for the customary cockroach crawl. He wheeled over the stool next to the bed and took a seat.

"Me again. Remember, it's once for no and twice for yes," he told the patient. The patient blinked twice.

"I'll ask you again. Is there anyone I can call for you?"

Blink.

"Please try to think harder. We really have to get you out of here. This last time you relapsed into coma, there was a lot of pressure from the Boss to pull the plug. The state is responsible for your care and they don't have no money, which means we won't get no reimbursing! It's expensive to keep you hooked up. All this equipment costs a shitload of do-re-me."

The patient stared at the ceiling. All that came to the patient's mind was that this aide now had more cleavage than the last time he was here.

"I'm here to help you. Please give me a phone number. Now, bear with me. I know I may be repeating myself, but sometimes you remember what we have talked about and other times you don't. I told you already that we're not set up for e-mail here. Now, a phone number, please."

Blink.

"Lordy. At least give me a name now. You have enough strength today, so give me the first letter of the person's first name that we are writing to," the aide said, making eye contact with the patient and gesturing grandly toward the alphabet chart.

On the fifth box of the chart the patient blinked. It took a lot of effort.

"E?"

Blink. Blink.

THE END

Acknowledgements

Thank you to my husband Richard, for all the time he spent helping me shape this pile of words into something worth reading. I'm grateful to Joan Teel, Laura Morton, Bernadine Styburski, Nancy Teel and Christine Teel for their eye opening feedback during this process. I am enamored of this beautiful city Los Angeles, my home, and my muse, without which this story could never have been written.

About the Author

K.T. Waltzer loves reading great thrillers and recently discovered that she also loves writing them. As a Los Angeles interior designer she assembles elements to shape a space. Similarly, as a writer, she links words together to tell a story. What better backdrop than the high-end interior design world in Los Angeles to be home to her debut novel, Catfight. Waltzer lives in Southern California with her husband.

Dad